LOCAL YOKELS

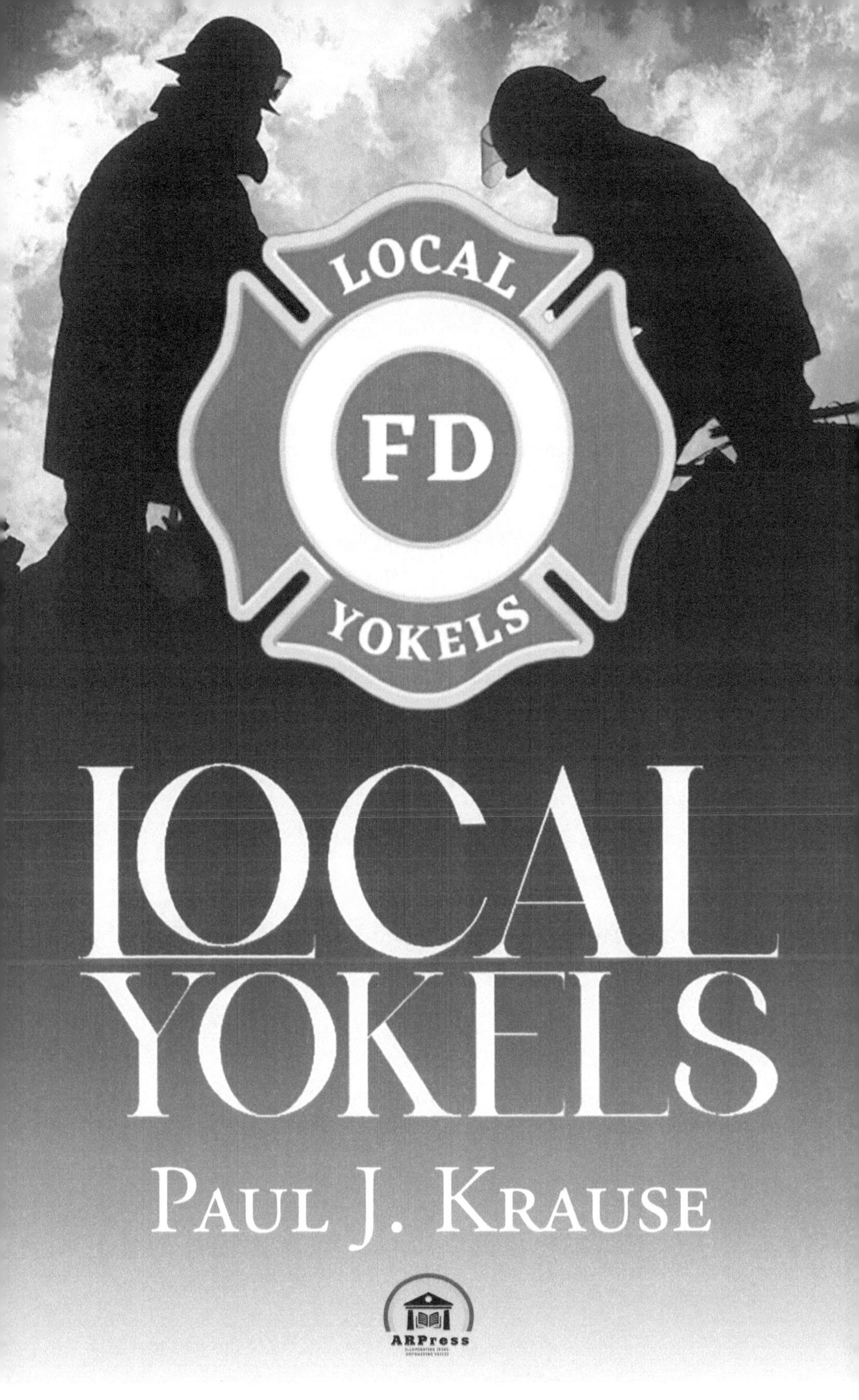

LOCAL YOKELS

PAUL J. KRAUSE

ARPress
45 Dan Road Suite 5
Canton MA 02021
Hotline: 1(888) 821-0229
Fax: 1(508) 545-7580

Ordering Information:

Quantity sales. Special discounts are available on quantity purchases by corporations, associations, and others. For details, contact the publisher at the address above.

Printed in the United States of America.

ISBN-13:   Softcover   979-8-89356-417-4

                eBook   979-8-89356-416-7

                Hardcover   979-8-89356-418-1

Library of Congress Control Number: 2024904688

TABLE OF CONTENTS

Chapter 1

It was a warm Monday morning. The June sun was shining and a light breeze cooled the summer air. A blue jay sat on a branch chirping outside Bootknife's window. With a full body jerk, Bootknife sat straight up in bed. Soaked and breathing heavily, he took a second to look around his room and realized that he was in his house.

"Damn nightmares," he gasped.

Pealing the sweaty sheets off of his legs, Bootknife pushed them to the end of his bed and swung his legs over the side of his mattress. He let them hang there for a few seconds before placing his feet on the hardwood floor. The floor creaked as he stood up. Stretching, he glanced at the alarm clock, sitting on the edge of his dresser. The red numbers showed 6:45am.

The phone, on the nightstand, rang, startling him a little bit. Ring, Ring. Ring, Ring.

"I'm coming. I'm coming. Hello?"

"What's up mother fucker?" The voice on the other end was the familiar one of Slim.

"Yeah?"

"We still meeting at the FD at seven thirty?"

"Yeah."

"Roger that! Did I wake you up?"

"No."

"Ok. See ya down there," Slim said.

"Yeah. Hey, remember that you got breakfast today." It was Slim's turn to buy breakfast. The two meet at the firehouse every Monday morning to go over the apparatus with the full-timers and make sure all of the equipment is in service for the upcoming week.

"Yeah, yeah. I got it." Slim laughed.

"Later." Bootknife hung up the phone and headed to the bathroom. Fifteen minutes later, he was showered and shaved and ready to get the day started. He put on a pair of khaki cargo shorts and a fire department t-shirt then headed downstairs to grab his sneakers.

Traffic was a nightmare at that time of morning. Between people trying to get to work and school buses trying to get kids to school, the avenue was backed up as far as the eye could see. Bootknife sighed, turned the radio up and threw his head back on the headrest. His 2008 Dodge Charger rumbled as it sat idling at the traffic light. Horns honked and people grew more and more impatient as traffic continued to stand still. Bootknife just laughed in amazement at how ridiculous the traffic was, as well as out of a little frustration.

Bootknife pulled into the firehouse parking lot right behind Slim. Slim put his Sonoma into the first parking spot, closest to the building, and sat there while he waited for the song that was playing to end. He took one last drag on the cigarette hanging on the end of his lips, and then flicked the cherry off just before it hit the filter. Bootknife pulled in next to him and got out of his car. Lighting a cigarette, he leaned into the open passenger-side window of Slim's truck.

"I see you have a new scrape on the side of your truck bed. Where'd you get that?"

Slim replied chuckling, "I got that at the jobsite, Friday. Hit my Dad's van going to get coffee for everyone."

"You really know how to keep this thing looking mint," Bootknife joked, snatching the Dunkin Donuts bag off of the seat. After finishing his smoke, Bootknife and Slim headed into the firehouse to eat. Beamer and Big'n'Rich were sitting in the radio room, each working on different things on the two computers. Beamer looked up from entering names into the firehouse software program, from the stack of roll calls for the medical and fire calls over the weekend.

"Looks like you guys had a busy weekend here," Beamer said.

"Mostly the usual though. Nothing too exciting," Bootknife replied. The three full-timers, Beamer, Big'n'Rich, and Grey, didn't work on the weekend. They worked Monday through Friday, between 6am and 5pm. Big'n'Rich worked the 6am to 2pm shift, Beamer worked 7am to 3pm, and Grey worked 9am to 5pm. Big'n'Rich loved the 6am to 2pm shift because it gave him almost the whole afternoon to drive up to Maine on Fridays during the summer.

"Slim, you hungry?" Beamer asked.

"Fuckin' A, man." Slim was barely able to get those three words out in between bites. He picked up two sausage, egg, and cheese bagel sandwiches and two orders of hash browns for himself.

"I think I can hear you getting fatter," Bootknife said. "What are you tipping the scale at these days? Two Seventy Five? Two Eighty?"

"Just remember, it takes a real man to build a shed over his tool," Slim fired back.

Beamer grabbed his breakfast from the kitchen and joined Bootknife and Slim at the table. The weather was on the T.V. and looked like the temperature was going to reach 90 today. "Today's going to suck if we get a fire!" Bootknife said, chewing the last bite of his bagel. Beamer and Slim both agreed. It had been a couple months since there was a fire in town, so everyone had been talking about how they were due for a good worker.

After the three were done eating, they cleaned up the table, threw out their trash, and headed out to the apparatus bay to begin checking the two engines and the rescue. Since each person took a different piece of apparatus, the checks didn't take long. They were finished by 9am, just as Grey pulled in to start his shift. Grey started chatting with Slim when the dispatcher came over the radio. Grey, Slim, Beamer, and Bootknife stood in front of the firehouse listening intently to see who was getting the call. "East Side and Headquarters, you're responding to the wreck on I-Eighty Four, at Exit Thirty Nine, with minor injuries." The tones went off and the dispatcher repeated the same message.

"Damn man. Today's going to be dead down here. We never get anything when the other side of town gets first blood." Grey looked a little disappointed while saying this. He kicked a stone into the catch basin and walked inside to put his lunch in the fridge. Right before he walked through the door, he looked back and shouted, "I'm going to drop a heater, so come get me if there's a call." Grey had just finished and was washing his hands when Slim came running into the bathroom.

"Let's go!" Slim shouted. "We got a report of a fire on the second floor of the apartments down by the high school!"

Grey wiped his hands on his pant legs and ran out to the apparatus bay. Big'n'Rich was starting Engine 5 as Grey stepped into his boots and pulled up his bunker pants. Throwing his jacket over his shoulder and grabbing his helmet from the top of his locker, he joined Slim and Bootknife in the back of the rig. Beamer looked back from the officer's seat and asked if everyone was ready to go.

"Let's do this." Slim said as he pulled his nomex hood over his head. He grabbed Bootknife's and Grey's identification tags, clipped them to his, and handed them up to Beamer. Slim looked at Grey and Bootknife and said, "I got the Irons!"

"I'll grab the knob. Grey you want to back me up?" asked Bootknife.

"I got your back buddy."

It was a straight shot from the firehouse to the apartments, which were about a mile down the road. Thick black smoke could be seen blowing across the avenue as they came around the soft corner about a quarter mile from the scene. Dispatch gave an update stating they had received multiple calls so far. As Big'n'Rich pulled the engine into the parking lot of the apartment complex, Beamer got on the radio and placed them on scene. "Base, Engine Five is on scene. Two story wood frame, heavy smoke and fire showing from two windows on the number two floor." Beamer threw the hand mic off to the side, grabbed the thermal imaging camera and jumped out of the rig.

Slim was checking the door that went to the stairwell of the apartment, to see if it was unlocked. Bootknife was flaking out the 2-1/2 inch hose line, while Grey was hooking the front 5-inch supply line to the hydrant for Big'n'Rich. Beamer got on the hand radio and told the Tower Ladder from Headquarters to pull behind Engine 5, upon arrival, ladder the roof, and start ventilation. Grey opened the hydrant and then joined Slim, Beamer, and Bootknife, who were putting on their masks at the door. When they were all ready, Grey and Bootknife led the way up the stairs with the uncharged hose line. Beamer and Slim were close behind. The heat was fairly intense when they reached the landing on the stairs between the first and second floor. The orange-red glow of the fire could be seen through the thick smoke at the top of the stairs. Bootknife held everyone up on the landing and Beamer called for Big'n'Rich to charge the line.

Big'n'Rich pulled the lever on the pump and the hose whip around as the water rushed through it. He got on the radio, "Water's on its way!" The Tower Ladder had arrived and two guys got in the bucket and raised it to the roof to start venting. Engine 2 had arrived on scene behind the Tower Ladder, and the operator, Sly, was working with Big'n'Rich to lay into Engine 5 so they could be supplied with water as well. Engine 2's crew, consisting of Doc, who is Bootknife's twin, Shakes and Big Deve, took a 1-3/4-inch hose line up the stairs to the apartment next to the fire apartment to start checking for extension. The Chief had also arrived on scene and was on the radio giving Engine 6, from Headquarters, and Rescue 15 from Uville, their assignments for when they arrived on scene.

Beamer gave Bootknife and Grey the heads up that water was on its way. Bootknife could feel the hose whipping around as the water made its way to the nozzle. He opened the bale a little to allow the air to escape. The water hit the nozzle, and Bootknife opened the bale all the way to let the water flow. He directed the stream towards the top of the stairs. After a few seconds, which felt like minutes to the crew, the fire at the top of the stairs had been knocked down enough to advance the line to the top and start hitting the main body of the fire. Bootknife closed the bale, and Grey and Beamer helped advance the heavy line up the rest of the stairs. Slim stayed on the landing to pull the line up the stairs to reduce the strain on the other three. Once enough hose was up in the hallway, on the second floor, Slim joined the other three on the fire floor.

"Damn it's hot," Slim thought as he rounded the corner on the fire floor. "This is definitely the hottest fire I've been in so far!" Beamer shouted back to Slim, telling him to search the first room on the right to make sure there were no victims. There had been no report of anyone being trapped, but every room gets searched no matter what. When people are panicking, they can forget to mention that someone else was in the house with them. The room was completely black. The smoke was still so thick that Slim couldn't see his hand in front of his mask. He moved quick, keeping his right foot against the wall, sweeping out in front of him with the halligan, feeling for a body. Every few feet Slim looked overhead to make sure there wasn't fire above him. The heat was intense, borderline unbearable. He felt like he was being baked in an oven. After going around the whole room, checking on top of, and behind, chairs and under tables, Slim made his way back out into the hallway to where the other three were fighting the fire. "Room checks clear!" he shouted to Beamer.

Bootknife was directing the water into the room, on the left, at the end of the hallway. The room was heavily involved, but the 300 gallons per minute that the 2-1/2 inch line was putting out, was knocking the fire down. Bootknife closed the bale one more time so they could push further into the room. He opened the bale and extinguished the remaining flames. The sounds of a roof saw could be heard overhead as the Tower Ladder was finishing cutting the vent holes in the roof above the fire. The smoke slowly started lifting from inside the room, and with the help of hand lights, Slim, Grey, Beamer, and Bootknife could begin to see around the room a little. Water could also be heard spraying above them. Just then, Engine 6's officer reported over the radio that they had a 1-3/4 inch hose line in operation extinguishing a small pocket of fire at the end of the cockloft.

Engine 2's crew reported no extension into the abutting apartment, but reported a smoke condition and was requesting vent fans to be brought up to the second floor. Rescue 15's crew came up to relieve Slim, Beamer, Grey, and Bootknife, to start overhauling the burned out apartment. The relief was welcomed by all four of them, who were not only exhausted from the high heat and strenuous work to extinguish the blaze, but they were all low on air and needed to get their bottles changed out. As the four exited the building, the air felt extremely refreshing even though the temperature outside was in the high 80s.

"Holy shit! Now that was a job," Bootknife said looking at Slim and Grey. Beamer reported to the Chief the conditions they had found on the fire floor, then the Chief had their whole crew go straight to rehab. Beamer, Grey, Slim, and Bootknife walked over to where Medic 12 from Headquarters had set up the rehab station. The four of them dropped their packs, coats, hoods and helmets on the ground next to the tarp and all but collapsed where they stood. They each chugged three bottles of water in about a minute, had their vitals assessed, and then just sat there for a few minutes, each with a huge grin on their faces. Their gear was blackened and covered in all sorts of debris. Their leather helmets were melted, with their brims curled up in some spots and drooping in others.

"Looks like you're going to need a new shield."

"You got that right, Slim." Bootknife looked at the hand carved shield on the front of his helmet. Before this fire, the shield still looked almost new. The green paint was now completely burned black. The once stiff shield had melted and folded over. It was no longer under the brass shield holder and was only being held on by the two screws lower on the helmet front. He was going to need to pull out one of the other shields, he had used previously, from the shadow box that hung on the wall in his room. There were a dozen shields hanging in it, which went back to when he was a Fire Cadet.

Once Engine 6's crew had extinguished the fire in the cockloft and overhaul was complete, Bootknife and Slim helped Big'n'Rich break the hydrant down and repack Engine 5. Once everything was back onboard, everyone got on the rig and headed back to the firehouse. The ride back was energetic and filled with chatter. All four of them had to fill Big'n'Rich in on the conditions inside the apartment and how hot it was. Big'n'Rich in turn reminisced on fires he had gone to when he was younger, when firefighters still rode on the back step of the Engines. "Those were different times, there boys," Big'n'Rich would say. He loved talking about fighting fires in the 70s.

When they pulled up back in front of the firehouse, cars were everywhere. This was a bit of a surprise seeing how the fire came in during the workday. Most of the time there is a skeleton crew between 7am and 4pm. Members do turn out for fires though, especially since there aren't as many fires these days. After all the apparatus was backed up to the firehouse, the equipment that was used was pulled off the rigs and cleaned. The hose lines were removed, hosed off, and repacked. Once everything was put back in service, it was time for lunch.

Chapter 2

ootknife got home and took off his clothes before going upstairs. His clothes were soaked and smelled of burned plastic and wood. He called this unique smell bunker funk, which was a mix of sweat, smoke, and other unknown odors that got trapped inside his turnout gear. He loved that smell. To him it smelled like hard work and a job well done. He dropped his clothes into the washer, picked up his wallet, pager, cell phone, and keys and headed to the shower.

It was hot in his room and he began sweating as soon as he walked into it. He was used to "second showers" as he referred to them. Seven months in Iraq will get you used to a lot when it comes to heat. He walked to the window, which overlooked the backyard, and turned the crank to open the window as wide as possible. He did this in the attempt to capture even a little bit of a breeze. This didn't happen though. The afternoon air had grown stagnant. No wind, high humidity and the thermometer peaking at 93 degrees made for a miserable day. Bootknife pulled the shade down about halfway, hoping to block a little heat from the sun, turned around and walked to his dresser to pull out a new set of clothes. It wasn't long before the new t-shirt was spotted with sweat marks.

The only thing that allowed Bootknife to not completely hate life in the heat, were the shades of green that made up his backyard. Every tree behind the house was full of lush green leaves, which created a fairly large shaded area in the back of his lot. After grabbing a cold bottle of water from the fridge, he walked into his living room, and crashed on the couch. Sipping the water, he looked out through the window and flashed back to when he was on a convoy in Iraq. They were on the North side of the Euphrates River, driving along a dirt road and off to the right were green fields that ran along the river's edge. This was the only area in their Area of Operation that was green like this. There were other areas they had driven through that had some green trees and a little grass, but that was only when they were along the river. Everything else was a light brown and tan color. Nothing but sand and stones as far as the eye could see.

"Base to all monitors, monthly meetings will be held at your respective stations tonight starting at nineteen hundred hours. Please make every effort to attend. Time out eighteen thirty." Bootknife's pager squelched for a few seconds then went silent. He rubbed his eyes and looked around. "I must have fallen asleep," he thought. Standing up, he stretched and made his way to the kitchen to see if he had any food in the fridge. A small container of mac and cheese was sitting on the middle shelf. He reached in, took the container out, wolfed the cheesy noodles down, and then left the house. It wasn't a good idea to miss a monthly meeting unless you had a good excuse.

When Bootknife pulled into the firehouse parking lot, there were only a couple spots left. There were five members standing outside the bays smoking and energetically talking about the fire today. One of the new guys was standing there asking questions about what happened since he was at work and missed the fire.

"You missed a good one!" said Doc.

Slim piped in with his usual, "Fuckin' A!" Followed by, "That was the best fire I've been to since I've been here."

Everyone agreed, dropped their finished cigarettes into the butt can, and started heading in to claim their seats for the meeting.

Bootknife told Slim to save a seat for him and headed into the bay to change the shield out on his helmet. He stashed the burnt up shield in his car, ran inside, and sat down as the gavel fell, marking the beginning of the meeting.

The meeting lasted for a little over an hour. It had consisted of the usual information and then discussion of the upcoming carnival. Nothing else was being brought before the company, so a motion to adjourn was made, seconded, and the gavel fell one last time. Everyone got up and made their way outside again where the smoking and joking continued. Everyone started to part around 9pm. This included Bootknife who had to run home to change and then head to work.

It was around 7:30am the next morning, when Bootknife arrived back in town. His shift at the bomb factory was uneventful, but seemed to go by pretty quickly. He swung by the firehouse to see what was going on there. Beamer and Big'n'Rich were in the same location as they had been the morning before.

"Anyone want anything for breakfast?" Bootknife asked.

"Where are you going?" asked Beamer.

"I was thinking about heading over to the café to get a breakfast sandwich to go."

"Yeah, I'll take a walk with you. Big'n'Rich, you good?"

"Yeaup." He said spinning around in his seat.

Beamer and Bootknife started walking to the café. They both checked to make sure their pagers were on as they left. "I still can't get over that shit yesterday," said Bootknife. "We'll probably not have another fire like that again for a while."

"Nope. That would be pretty sweet if we had something like the five fires in six days again, though. Honestly though I doubt that will happen," said Beamer.

"Yeah, no shit," Bootknife replied. "You know, there has been a lot of Line of Duty Deaths lately. Across the country there have been ten this month alone. I'm surprised this town hasn't ever had one. There have been some close calls in the past."

"You're right. Think about all the fires in the old days. When our fathers started, they used to fight fires without any breathing apparatus and sometimes without any gear. And they had some really big fires!"

"Yeah. I guess we've just been lucky. Hopefully that luck doesn't run out anytime soon."

"I hear ya. We've got a good bunch of guys down here who watch each other's backs. We'll be good brotha."

"Yeah. Yeah, you're right," said Bootknife, still thinking about it. He had had some bad feelings about not making it home when he was in Iraq, and he made it back without a scratch. He had to just keep reminding himself of that.

The day was heating up as they walked back with their breakfast in hand. It was supposed to be just as hot as the day before. The air conditioning in the firehouse felt nice as they sat and ate their meal. After picking up, Beamer went back to the computer to keep working on a project the Chief gave him. Bootknife headed home to get some shuteye. He sent his girlfriend a text message and was out cold as soon as his head hit the pillow.

It was just after noon when Bootknife's phone rang, waking him up. "Wake up fucker!" Slim said. "We're grilling up some steak tips for lunch. Get your ass down here!"

Bootknife was up immediately. The steak tips they always get are amazing, and his mouth was watering just thinking of them. After washing up and changing really quickly, he whipped into the back parking lot at the firehouse and grabbed the first spot he saw. Slim, Grey, and Beamer were standing next to the grill, and Doc and Shakes walked out the back door holding plates and utensils. The smell of barbeque and house marinated steak tips filled the air. "You're just in time. Meat's ready," Grey stated.

"Perfect," Bootknife stated, flicking his cigarette into the grass on the side of the firehouse. They all sat down and started eating. Bootknife was happy Slim had called him and gave him the heads up on this.

"Slim, you have a half day at work today?" Bootknife asked.

"Yeah. It was too hot to work by ten, so my Dad said fuck it."

"Fuckin' A! Good things man," Bootknife said as he was finishing his last bite of meat.

Everyone sat around outside for a bit, to digest a little, before picking up. Bootknife moved his car to the front of the firehouse and everyone went to lounge in the meeting room. The air conditioning was cranking now and everyone was content with remaining indoors. Just after Big'n'Rich left at 2pm, dispatch sounded the tones for a medical call. Doc, Grey, and Shakes took Medic 16, leaving Beamer, Slim, and Bootknife behind incase another call came in.

As Doc, Grey, and Shakes were on their way back, after getting a patient refusal, the tones hit, followed by the dispatcher's excited voice. "Base to Hose Company One and Headquarters, report of a fire in the basement at Fourteen Canton Creek Circle. Home is being evacuated at this time." Doc hit the switch for the lights, flipped the siren switch to yelp, and Grey put the gas pedal to the floor. They weaved and bobbed through traffic trying to get back to the firehouse. After getting slowed up a bit in the center of the village, Grey sped around the corner and parked the Medic off to the side so it was out of the way. The three ran in and grabbed their gear. Grey jumped in the driver seat of Engine 5, Beamer got into the officer seat, and Doc, Slim, Shakes, and Bootknife hopped in the back. The scene of the reported fire wasn't far from the firehouse, and they arrived in less than three minutes.

Beamer got on the radio on their arrival and reported heavy black smoke showing from the back of the house. Doc, Slim, and Shakes pulled a 1-3/4 inch cross lay and began stretching it to the back of the house. Bootknife reached up on top of the Engine and grabbed the 5-inch supply line and gave it a pull. There was a hydrant right on the edge of the property line about 15 feet away. He opened the hydrant, hooked the hose to it and charged it as soon as Grey was ready. After opening the hydrant, Bootknife grabbed a New York Hook and headed towards the back of the house, where the rest of the crew was. Along the way, Bootknife had been fixing the hose so when it was charged there would be no kinks in it, restricting the flow of water to the nozzle.

The smoke they saw on arrival was pouring out of the open hatchway. The homeowner stated he had just arrived home and heard an explosion in the basement right before he got through the door. He also said that he had been having some issues with his boiler the last couple days and had been waiting for a service technician to come out for a look. Beamer told him to go to the front of the house and wait by the street. Everyone had their masks on by then, and Doc bled the air out of the hose, as it was charged before making his way down the stairs to the basement. Slim and Shakes were close behind him, moving fast due to the amount of heat coming up the stairs. The stairway was like a large chimney, and no one wanted to be in there for very long. Beamer went next with Bootknife right behind him. The smoke was so thick that it was hard to locate the fire. Beamer looked through the thermal imaging camera and found the fire on the far side of the basement, behind what appeared to be a wall. As they got closer a glow could be seen.

Just before Doc opened the bale on the nozzle, Bootknife broke a couple windows as close to the fire as possible. The smoke and heat needed to have a way out as water was being put on the fire. If the heat couldn't be vented, there was a high probability of steaming the whole crew, which wouldn't be good. As soon as the windows had been broken, Doc opened the bale and started putting water on the fire. Using a large circle pattern typically works best when trying to extinguish a fire. A circle hits both high and low, side to side, and creates a vortex of sorts in the middle, choking the fire out.

It didn't take long before the fire had been put out. The Tower Ladder had arrived, and the crew went to the first floor of the house to check for extension and to start ventilating on that level. They found no extension but there was a pretty heavy smoke condition throughout the house. The Chief, who arrived just prior to the Tower, held the assignment to Engine 5, Engine 2 and the Tower Ladder. Doc moved the nozzle close to the window Bootknife broke out and using a narrow fog pattern, he hydraulically vented the basement. As the smoke cleared, it could be seen that the boiler had exploded and started the fire. Due to the quick response from the crew on Engine 5, the house was saved.

The smoke through the rest of the house was vented with the aid of vent fans. The cross lay was repacked by Slim and Shakes. Bootknife broke down the hydrant and repacked the section of 5 inch with Beamer. Everyone grabbed a bottle of water, got on the rig, and headed back to the firehouse. The fire hadn't been nearly as big as the one the day before, but it did drain the energy out of everyone, no thanks to the temperature outside. When they got back to the firehouse, there were a dozen guys standing around outside, ready to help with washing the cross lay and repacking it. Slim was using his head before they had left the fire and rinsed all the tools off prior to putting them back on the Engine.

"Two fires! Two fucking fires and I miss them! This is bullshit!" Killa walked out from behind the Rescue. He was pissed because he had been out of town the last two days finishing a construction project.

"Yeah, they were great!" Slim laughed. He always knew how to rub it in.

"I'm working up the road from here starting tomorrow, so I bet this run of fires is over. We never get anything good when I'm around," Killa said, a little less pissed.

Killa started to realize that he wasn't the only one who had missed the two fires. For both of them, Engine 3 had a full crew but never made it to the scene. The day before they had been relocated to Hose Company 1 and were canceled enroute for the fire that just happened. Those guys were pissed.

"We'll see you guys later. Time to get a nap in before work." Bootknife said.

"Hey, we'll see ya guy!" Killa shouted as Bootknife got into his car and left.

On the drive home, Bootknife couldn't help but wonder how long this streak was going to go on for. There have been multiple fires a week apart from each other, and the one time a few years before that there were five fires in six days. But, fires have usually been few and far between. "Hopefully just thinking about this doesn't jinx it," Bootknife thought to himself. Bootknife showered and shaved quickly then hopped into bed. When he woke up, it was twenty minutes before he was supposed to be at work. He threw his uniform on quickly and ran out the door. Fifteen minutes was more than enough time to make it to work, especially in his car.

Chapter 3

At 3pm, Bootknife pulled out of the bomb factory parking lot. It had been a long sixteen-hour shift but he didn't mind. One of the first shift guys needed a swap so he made out with an extra night off. The two shifts had been pretty much uneventful. A couple fire alarms came in during the middle of the night, but they were nothing exciting. While he had been at work, he missed a medical call and a minor car accident, but other than that it had been a slow day at the firehouse. It took him about thirty minutes to get back home due to the afternoon traffic, and the whole ride all he could think about was getting into bed for a quick nap. As soon as he got home, he parked his car in the garage, kicked his boots off, and fell into bed still in his work uniform, completely exhausted.

Bootknife didn't hear a sound until his phone rang at 7pm. The screen of the phone looked blurry, since he was still half asleep, but he was able to make out the name. It was Vera, his girlfriend. "Hello?" he said, in a hoarse voice.

"Hi baby! Did I wake you up?"

"Yeah, but it's okay. What's up?"

"Oh, sorry," she said, drawing out the word sorry. "I'm just getting off work and wanted to know if you wanted me to pick up dinner for you on my way over."

He had completely forgotten that she was coming over. "Umm, yeah if you don't mind. I don't have any food here at the house, so that would be great."

"Alrighty. What do you want?"

"It doesn't matter. Surprise me." Bootknife slurred his words a little as he began to nod off on the phone.

"Are you falling asleep on me?"

"No," he said, a little more alert now that he had been caught.

"You better not be. You better get up because I'll be there in a little bit."

"I will. I'm getting up now and going to jump in the shower."

"Sounds good. I'll see you soon. Bye."

As she hung up the phone, Bootknife let out a moan. He hated waking up. It was one of the hardest things for him to do since he got out of the Marines. The only time he was able to get right up and moving was when his pager went off, or if he woke up without an alarm after sleeping for at least eight hours. He loved sleep and felt like he rarely ever got completely caught up. He swung his left leg over the side of the bed and put his foot on the floor. He let it sit there for a few seconds as he rubbed his eyes, trying to clear up his vision. He finally swung his right leg off the bed and sat up. Sitting on the edge of his bed for a minute, he stretched and then stood up. A little uneasy on his feet still, he stripped off his uniform and stumbled down the hallway to the bathroom. He closed the door behind him and proceeded to shave, shower, and brush his teeth. Just as he finished getting dressed, he heard the door close downstairs and caught a whiff of one of his favorite things. He followed the aroma downstairs, around the corner, through the kitchen, and found Vera standing in the dining room holding a container with fried chicken, mashed potatoes with gravy, and green beans. She also had a second container full of mac and cheese.

"You's the bestest sho'ty!" he said jokingly with a huge smile on his face.

Vera responded, laughing, "I know. You don't need to keep reminding me."

Bootknife laughed, gave her a kiss, and took the food from her, as Vera went to put her overnight bag upstairs. Vera was a vegetarian, so he knew she was going to eat most of the mac and cheese, but he still stole a small scoop, because it just smelled way too good not to. On her way back through the kitchen, Vera grabbed a couple bottles of water from the fridge and came into the dining room to join him.

They made it through dinner without any interruptions, which was a nice change. Because of working third shift, they didn't get to sit down for dinner together often. After cleaning up, they went to the living room and started looking through the TV menu to see what was on. The selection wasn't great, so they ended up putting in a DVD. Just as the movie started, Bootknife's pager went off. Usually, he wouldn't leave for a call if Vera was over, unless it was something good, or if he hadn't been on call in a while. "Base to Hose Company One and Headquarters, structure fire at Two Londonberry Place." As soon as the dispatcher said "structure," Bootknife gave Vera a quick kiss and said, "Got to go!"

As he ran out of the room, Vera yelled from behind, "Be careful!" She sounded concerned, but at the same time, she wasn't surprised that he had to run out. There's usually at least one call that he has to go on when they get together after not seeing each other for a couple days.

Bootknife opened the garage door, turned on the blue lights in his car, and floored it out of the driveway. There weren't many cars on the road, and he caught green lights at each of the three traffic lights between his house and the firehouse. When he pulled into the parking lot, Big Deve was right on his bumper. Bristol pulled in behind him and Slim arrived next. Bootknife ran through the front door of the firehouse and into the bay. As he was pulling his bunker pants up, he heard the Chief come over the radio reporting heavy fire showing from the front of the house, and also reported a child was still in the house. Everyone started moving quicker. Bootknife's brother Loo pulled in, and the five of them jumped on the rig and pulled out. Big Deve had to slam on the brakes at the end of the parking lot as Shakes pulled in. Big Deve turned the corner out of the parking lot and put the pedal to the metal.

"Bristol and Bootknife, you two are going to do a search when we get there, Slim, you're with me on the line!" Loo shouted from the officer's seat.

A round of "Ten-Fours" came from the back as Slim, Bristol, and Bootknife put their air packs on and grabbed hand lights. When they arrived, they found a split-level ranch with fire coming out of two windows and running across the siding on the front of the house. As soon as Big Deve stopped the rig, everyone jumped into action. Bootknife grabbed a hook and a water-can, Bristol grabbed the set of irons and Slim and Loo started stretching the line. The Chief said the parents reported the child was in the last room on the right. Bristol and Bootknife ran around to the back of the house, where they found the back door open. They masked up and radioed to the Chief that they were entering the building. As they went in, Slim and Loo were reaching the back door with the hose, which still needed to be charged.

Upon entering the house, Bristol and Bootknife were swallowed up in thick, black smoke. The heat grew more intense as they made their way through the kitchen toward the hallway. The living room, which is attached to the kitchen and dining room in this type of house, was fully involved. Slim and Loo had to get water on that fire soon or their path back would become blocked, trapping them with the victim. As they crawled past the wall of fire in the living room, and started working their way into the hallway, they gritted their teeth as the left side of their bodies felt like it was going to melt off. As they entered the hallway they couldn't see anything. The smoke was so thick, that they knew no one could survive long, and moved a lot faster. As they came up on the first room on the right, Bristol checked the door for heat, swung it open and yelled, "Fire Department! Is there anyone in here?" He conducted a right hand search quickly, but thoroughly, and came up with nothing. When he came close to the door, he told Bootknife to move on to the next room. Bootknife crawled past the door and Bristol followed behind him. When they reached the next door, the last one on the right, Bootknife found it open. There was no visible fire in the room, so he left the water-can at the doorway and made entry. The heat was going up every second, from the growing fire down the hall. The hissing of the hose and noises of fire being extinguished could not be heard yet. "Fire Department! Is anyone in here?" Bootknife shouted and continued to repeat as he searched around the room for the boy who was supposed to be in there.

About half way through the search, Bristol yelled into the room, "The line ruptured in the front yard. They're working on replacing it now so it's going to be a few before they can get water on the bitch!" He began looking around again, after passing that information to Bootknife, checking the conditions above, beside, and behind him. The glow behind them was growing brighter and the heat was really starting to go up. He pulled the pin out of the water-can, pointed the hose toward the ceiling and gave it a few blasts. The glow darkened for a couple seconds and then began to grow again. "Our exit is blocked! The fire's running down the hallway!" he shouted in to Bootknife, who had just located the missing boy.

"I got 'em! He's barely breathing!" Bootknife shouted to Bristol.

Bristol crawled into the room and closed the door behind him. He got on the radio, trying to remain calm, calling the Chief, "Engine Five Search to Command, Urgent!"

"Command's on, go search!"

"Chief, the fire is making a run down the hallway. Our exit is blocked and we have the victim. He's barely breathing. We need a ladder to the window on the C-B corner, fast!"

"Roger! We have RIT on their way!"

Bootknife dragged the victim to the wall, under the window, and yelled to Bristol, "Control that door buddy! I'm going to break the window!"

"Go for it!" Bristol yelled back.

Bootknife brought his hand up to the side of his face and groped around for the plastic quick release for the chinstrap. As soon as he located it, he unbuckled it, removed his helmet and threw it at the window as hard as he could. The sound of the glass breaking was a comforting sound. Now the RIT team knew exactly what window to throw the ladder to. About fifteen seconds later, there was the sound of more breaking glass and Bootknife could feel it hitting the back of his coat, as he laid over the victim, protecting him as much as possible from the increasing temperature in the room. Just as the tip of the aluminum ladder was heard hitting the windowsill, Bristol yelled to Bootknife, "The water can is running low and the door's burning through!"

"Thirty seconds! Hold it for thirty more seconds!" Bootknife yelled back as he raised the victim off the floor and slung his, now limp, body over the top rung of the ladder.

"I got him, maaann!" came Killa's voice, from just outside the window. Bootknife couldn't see him due to all the smoke billowing out the window.

"He's no longer breathing!" Bootknife yelled out to Killa. "Bristol, come on! We're bailing out!"

Bristol left the empty water can at the door and crawled as fast as he could, across the room, to the window. Half of the door was burned away now and flames were rolling across the ceiling. Bootknife grabbed Bristol's pack strap and pulled it towards the ladder. "Go!" he shouted. Bristol grabbed the top rung of the ladder and went head first out the window.

"I got you brother!" said Doc, right as Bristol came over the top rung.

Just as Bristol's feet cleared the tip of the ladder, Bootknife came out headfirst. He was moving faster now as the flames were racing across the room and licked the bottom of his boots as his feet cleared the window. Right before Bootknife face-planted into the ground, he felt someone grab the waist belt on his pack, which stopped him. When he looked up, he saw Farley's face. "Thanks Farley! Smashing into the ground would have sucked!"

Farley laughed, a nervous laugh, and helped him up. "You guys ok?"

"Ya, just dandy! How's the vic?" Bootknife said.

"Not sure. They took him around front to the ambulance. You sure you're ok?"

"Ya, fine. Just another day!" Bootknife pulled his hood back and removed his mask. "Bristol, you good?"

Bristol was the quiet type, so it didn't surprise anyone when he only answered, "Ya." He had his typical smirk on his face.

"RIT from Command, is Engine Five search accounted for?"

"Roger that Chief. They're out of the building. They will be heading around front for evaluation in a second." Doc released the mic and started moving everyone around to the front.

Just before Bootknife got to the front of the house, Killa came running up to him. "Bootknife maaannn! You're fucking crazy maaaannnn!"

"Na man!" Bootknife said laughing.

Bootknife and Bristol were evaluated at the scene and were told they couldn't go back inside. They stood next to the ambulance for the remainder of the fire. The house ended up being a total loss. The fire marshal came out and at the end of his investigation ruled it as arson. The victim's condition was still unknown.

Chapter 4

The ride back to the firehouse was a quiet one. Everyone was reflecting on what happened at the fire and really wasn't in the mood to talk. As they backed up the driveway, the firefighters who had been standing by at the firehouse were outside, eagerly waiting to hear what happened. Word spread that Bristol and Bootknife were the individuals trapped. Beamer had heard and called Vera. She was standing next to Beamer and Grey, and as soon as the engine stopped and Bootknife got stepped off it, she ran up to him and threw her arms around his neck. She squeezed him as hard as she could. Tears began to roll down her cheeks as he put his arms around her and hugged her back saying, "I'm okay. Don't cry. Really I'm okay."

Bootknife looked at Beamer, remembering the conversation they had the other day, "Close call tonight." That's all he had to say. Beamer nodded his head. He knew exactly what Bootknife was talking about.

Slim thought about cracking a joke as he stepped off the engine behind Bootknife, but after what had just happened, he kept it to himself. Vera finally released Bootknife and allowed him to go take his gear off. Beamer and Grey kept her distracted as Bootknife and the others took tools off the rig to wash down, and add more hose to replace the length that had burst, so they could get back in service. As soon as everything was put away, everyone signed in and then made their way outside. It didn't take long before the front of the firehouse had a huge cloud of smoke lingering in front of it. At first everyone was fairly quiet, but then Slim broke the silence. "Sorry guys." he said softly.

"Don't say that!" Bootknife snapped. "It wasn't your fault that shit went downhill. The hose burst and there's nothing you could have done to prevent that."

"We got out in one piece Slim. We're ok!" Bristol said.

Luckily Killa was ready to lighten the mood a little and chimed in. "You guys are fucking crazy maaann! Fuckin' A, maaann!" He laughed, which became contagious and everyone else laughed too. Vera even laughed. She had her arms wrapped around his left arm and was standing right up against him. She didn't want to let him go after almost losing him earlier.

The Chief walked out and told the crowd that he had just gotten a phone call from the paramedics who took the victim in to the hospital. They had got him breathing before they reached the hospital, and the doctors were saying he should make a full recovery. Everyone let out a sigh of relief.

All the smokers lit one more cigarette and the Chief lit one of his cigarillos. As they finished smoking they walked to their cars and began heading home. They were all still riding the adrenalin rush from the fire, but were emotionally exhausted.

Bootknife turned into his driveway, Vera right behind him, put his car into the garage and they headed upstairs. "What a night!" he said to her.

"Let's not talk about it. My heart sank when I got the call from Beamer."

"I'm sure it did. Bristol and I had it under control," he said with a smirk.

"Like I said, let's not talk about it. I'm just glad you're alright! Go get in the shower. You stink!"

"I'm going, I'm going," Bootknife said laughing.

After he dried off, Bootknife put on a pair of gym shorts and a t-shirt, brushed his teeth, and jumped into bed. Vera wrapped her arms around him, planted a long kiss on his cheek and said, "Don't scare me like that again! Ok?"

"Okay."

"Promise?"

"I promise."

With that Bootknife rolled over and shut off the light. As soon as he shut his eyes he was out cold. The dreams started almost immediately. Bootknife fought to save himself and Bristol all over again. As he tossed and turned, Vera shook him. He woke with a shudder. Breathing heavy and sweating profusely, he looked around the darkened room.

"You okay?" Vera asked.

"Ya. Fine. Go back to sleep."

Bootknife laid back down as Vera snuggled up against him. He lay on his back, wide awake for about an hour thinking about the fire. He was thankful that there had been a good crew outside. He and Bristol would have been crispy critters if it wasn't for them.

Bootknife and Vera were woken up by the alert tone on the pager. After the second set of tones finished, the dispatcher came across the speaker, "Hose Company One and Headquarters, report of a dryer fire Sixteen High Road. House is being evacuated at this time. Six-Oh-Five."

Bootknife was running down his stairs as the dispatcher was finishing the dispatch. Bootknife sped out of his driveway, screeching the tires as he turned onto his street. "Here we go again!" he mumbled.

Vera had gotten up right after Bootknife had pulled out, and turned the scanner up downstairs so she could listen to the call. She started to worry a little, still shaken after the events of last night.

When Bootknife pulled into the firehouse, Big'n'Rich was pulling Engine 5 out. He ran inside, kicked off his sneakers, pulled on his bunker pants, grabbed his helmet and jacket and ran out to the rig. Killa, Shakes, and Doc were pulling in as he exited the bay. Bootknife climbed into the officer seat as the other three were putting on their gear. They climbed in the back of the engine and Bootknife told Big'and'Rich, "Hit it!" Bootknife stepped on the pedal and wound up the siren, gave the air horn a couple long blasts to clear the intersection, and signed on responding.

"Killa, when we get there, grab a watercan and the irons. Doc and Shakes, stretch a line to the hatchway, if there is one." Bootknife said looking into the back at them.

"Roger!" They all replied.

As they pulled up, the homeowner was on the front lawn flagging them down. "Engine Five's on the scene. Single story wood frame. Light smoke coming from the front door. We're checking." Bootknife reported to dispatch. Before dismounting, he reached over and grabbed the thermal imaging camera.

"Killa, you're with me! We're going to see what we got. Doc and Shakes, I'll let you know if we're going to need the line." Bootknife shouted so they could hear him over the roar of the engine.

Bootknife and Killa found a light smoke condition on the first floor as they worked towards the downstairs door in the kitchen. When Killa reached the door, he checked it for heat with his backhand and opened it. There was a decent amount of smoke coming from all around the door prior to opening it. As soon as Killa turned the knob and pulled the door open, thick smoke began billowing out into the kitchen. Killa shut the door and they both masked up. Right before they opened the door, Doc came over the radio. "Five nozzle to five officer."

Bootknife keyed up the hand mic, "Go five nozzles."

"Five officer, be advised, we have reached the hatchway and it's locked from the inside. It's in the middle of the Charlie side. We can see a small fire through the basement window. Looks like it may still be contained to the dryer."

"Ten-Four. We're making entry to the basement now. We'll open the hatchway for ya when we get down there."

Killa opened the door again and they began descending the stairs. The smoke was thick but there wasn't a lot of heat, which was a good thing. When they reached the bottom, they could see a glow to the right. They turned the corner and saw a perfect circle of fire. Killa made his way over to the flames, set down the irons, pulled the pin on the water can and began extinguishing the fire. Bootknife looked through the thermal imager to check for any extension to the wall behind the dryer or on the underside of the floor above it. There was a slight elevation in temperature on the wall and up above, but it wasn't high enough for either to be burning. Bootknife turned to his right looking through the thermal imager and saw what appeared to be the entrance to the hatchway. He walked over to it, climbed a couple stairs, unlocked the hatchway and threw it open. The smoke began pushing out of the basement and to the outside. He saw Doc and Shakes there with the stretched line. "Leave the hose there and come down to help open some windows." Bootknife said.

Bootknife turned around, and while walking back down the hatchway stairs, keyed up the hand mic. He radioed the Chief, who had arrived just as Killa began extinguishing the fire. "Engine Five to Command."

"Command answering."

"Chief, fire has been knocked down with a water can. No extension seen through the thermal imager. We still have a pretty heavy smoke condition and are going to need a couple fans for ventilation. We're opening some windows down here as we speak."

"Command copies." The Chief radioed dispatch and had all apparatus responding go with the flow of traffic. He cancelled Engine 6, and kept Engine 2 and the Tower Ladder coming to assist with venting. The Tower arrived on scene right after Bootknife gave the Chief his report. The Tower's crew took two fans off the truck and brought one to the front door and one to the hatchway.

When the Lieutenant from the Tower got to the top of the hatchway steps he saw Bootknife and yelled down to him, "Local Yokels, Maaaann!"

Bootknife looked up and saw Patty. Patty was a Lieutenant out of Headquarters. The two of them grew up together and were practically brothers. "What's up brother?" Bootknife replied.

"I got your fan for ya. You want it down there at the bottom?"

"Yeah, that would be great. See if you can get it hung up here in the door. Thanks Patty!"

"You got it brotha. Hey did you see the paper this morning?"

"No. Why what's up?"

"Some idiot from the next town over wrote something to the paper about the fire the other day at the apartments. They published it in the paper. You have to read it. Look for the column titled, Local Yokels Shut Down The Avenue."

"I'll check it out when we get back to the firehouse. Is it any good?"

"It'll get your blood boiling," he said with a chuckle.

"Excellent! Hey did Engine Two get here yet?"

"Yeah, they pulled up behind us as we were bringing the fans over."

"Was Slim on there?"

"He was riding shoty. He looked pissed. Haha. Must be since you guys put the fire out and he didn't get to go play."

"I bet I'll hear all about it back at the station." Bootknife laughed and then went to check on how much smoke was left in the basement. A couple minutes later the smoke was completely cleared from the basement and the upstairs. The fans were removed and the two crews walked out of the house.

Bootknife walked up to the Chief and said, "Chief. Everything's good inside. We pulled the dryer away from the wall and unplugged it from the outlet."

"Ok. As soon as you guys get everything back on the Engine, go ahead and clear. Nice work."

"Thanks." Bootknife checked to make sure Killa, Doc, and Shakes were all set, and then they mounted up and headed back to the firehouse. As they passed the Tower, Bootknife pulled twice on the chord for the air horns and threw up a wave at Patty. "What do ya think, there Big'n'Rich, we gonna get another job today or will this be it?"

Big'n'Rich shrugged his shoulders, "I don't know. I wouldn't mind a quiet day today."

"You wheel-manning it today?"

"Yeaup!"

"So you wouldn't mind wheeling us to another fire later right?"

"Doesn't matter to me."

"Fuckin', A!" Bootknife replied.

Chapter 5

When they got back to the station, there wasn't much to clean up. All that was really needed was to remove the used air bottles and refill the water can. As Bootknife rounded the front of the Engine, Slim started in on him.

"Had to take another fire by its balls, huh?" said Slim chuckling.

"Well you wanted to drag ass getting down here, so yeah."

"Drag ass? Haha, I had the pedal to the floor the whole way."

"Well, I think it's time you get rid of the golden turd and get something that actually does faster than sixty miles per hour."

"It does sixty…five, on a good day." Slim laughed, stepping outside of the bay to light a cigarette.

Bootknife went to hang up his gear in his locker and then signed in. He walked out front to join Slim and Shakes in a smoke. Beamer pulled into the driveway and grabbed the last spot. There wasn't a huge showing for this fire since most of the guys were getting ready for work.

Beamer walked up to the gang in front of Engine 5's bay and said, "You guys burn the house down?"

"Whoa, Whoa. This isn't the East Side. We run shit around here," Slim said laughing.

"Zing! One point Slim! Haha." Beamer walked into the firehouse and put his lunch in the fridge. He then came back outside and got the low down on dryer fire from the guys as they finished their cigarettes.

Bootknife walked inside to check the paper, remembering what Patty had mentioned to him. When he found the article, he read it and started a slow burn. "Who the fuck does this ass hole think he is? Slim, come check this shit out!"

Slim, Shakes, Doc, Beamer, and Killa all came over to the table to see what Bootknife was yelling about. They all crowded around, looking over each other's shoulder to read the article. Shakes piped up first. "What an ass hole."

Everyone else had a similar reaction. The article was about how this guy was all pissed off that he ended up being late to work because the fire department had shut down a section of the Avenue at the apartment fire the other day. He had to take the long way to work, which added fifteen minutes onto his travel time.

"Fuck him!" Beamer said.

Bootknife started laughing and said to the group, "I think we have a new nickname for ourselves boys. Local Yokels!"

"Haha, that's perfect!" Slim said. "Doc, can you create a new patch for us? A Local Yokel patch?"

Everyone laughed. Doc had an artistic side to him and he had created a couple patches over the last two or three years. Slim also had an artistic side, but he specialized in using the computer to create funny pictures. Slim and Bootknife looked at each other at the same time, thinking the same thing. Slim and Bootknife headed to the office and got onto the computer. Slim pulled up a picture of the IAFF patch and started messing around with it.

As they were working on the picture, the firehouse phone rang and Big'n'Rich answered. "Chief! Line one." Big'n'Rich put the caller on hold and hung up the phone. About ten minutes later, the Chief came out of his office.

"Slim, Bootknife, Killa, can I see you in my office?"

Slim looked at Bootknife and whispered, "What did we do? I don't think we did anything stupid lately."

Bootknife shrugged his shoulders and let the other two into the Chief's office and closed the door. "What's going on Chief?"

"The hospital just called and said the boy you guys saved last night is conscious now and has been asking for you."

"Umm, Chief, I didn't really do much to save that kid." Slim said, still feeling shitty about what happened with the hose.

"Shut up Slim!" Bootknife said jokingly. "He's been asking for us?"

"Yeah, he told his mother that he wanted to meet the guys who rescued him. The doctor I spoke to said you could come over now if you wanted."

"We'll head over there. I'm sure these guys don't have anything more important going on this morning."

The three walked out of the office. They were going to go home and shower quick then meet at Bootknife's house so they could take one car.

Slim and Killa got to Bootknife's house about forty-five minutes later. Bootknife was outside finishing a cigarette when they pulled in. He ran up to his back door and shouted in to Vera, "We're heading out. Call me when you get out of work!" They got into Bootknife's Charger and left for the hospital.

Bootknife pulled the car into the visitor lot at the hospital and parked it out in an empty part of the lot. He hated parking near other cars since he was so anal about keeping his car looking good. It had been hit by a lady who left her door open in the middle of a rainstorm. He had almost killed her, but kept himself under control enough to just tell the lady to get the hell out of there.

"Could you have parked any farther away?" Slim said laughing.

"Fuck you! I'm doing this for you. You could use a little exercise!"

"Was that a fat joke?" Slim said still chuckling.

"Take it however you want."

The three got out and walked towards the main entrance. They were all silent as they walked, but they stopped just before they got to the door. They looked at each other and Killa said, "Anyone else feel a little awkward?"

"A little bit." Slim said.

"Come on. Let's get this over." Bootknife replied.

They felt like anything but heroes. They did what they did because it was their job. They talked to the girl at the front desk and asked for the kid's room number. The girl looked it up and wrote it down for them. As they turned and began walking away, the girl said to them, "They've been waiting for you!" Bootknife turned and smiled at her, nodded his head and kept walking. They took the elevator to the sixth floor. The girl at the front desk must have called up to the room to give them a heads up that they had arrived because the boy's mother was waiting in front of the elevator as the doors opened. She hugged all three of them, thanking each one as she hugged them. She then led them down the hallway towards the recovery room.

When they walked into the room, the boy, Tommy looked over at them, and a huge smile lit up his face as his mother introduced them to him. The three were a little hesitant about moving farther into the room. They weren't exactly sure what to do. Bootknife took the initiative to be the first to move to Tommy's bedside. Slim and Killa slowly moved behind him and made their way around to the other side of the bed.

"Are you the guys who saved me?" Tommy asked. His voice was hoarse and just above a whisper.

"Yeah." Bootknife said. Not sure what else to say, he gave Tommy a smile and waited for the next question.

"Thank you." Tommy said. A tear appeared in the corner of his right eye, which almost immediately ran down his cheek.

"You're welcome." Bootknife replied softly.

Slim looked at Tommy and said, "These two guys are the ones who really saved you. Bootknife found you, and Killa was the one who took you from Bootknife and brought you down the ladder to the ambulance."

Tommy sat up slowly, and gave Bootknife and Killa each a hug.

Killa was finally able to get some words out and asked Tommy, "So how are you feeling?" He didn't know what else to say.

Tommy laid back down and looked at Killa, "I feel really tired and get a bad cough every once in a while. I've been sicker though."

"Well, we all hope you feel better soon. When you get out of here, feel free to stop by the firehouse anytime you want. We'll show you the rigs when you come," Bootknife said to Tommy.

"Wow, really?"

"Absolutely!" Killa replied.

"We're going to get going so you can rest up." Bootknife said to Tommy.

His mother grabbed Bootknife's arm and asked, "Can I get a picture of you guys with him before you leave?"

"Sure," Bootknife said.

Bootknife, Killa, and Slim moved to the head of the bed and got as close as possible to Tommy. His mother snapped the picture and checked it to make sure it came out ok.

"Thank you so much. I can't even begin to tell you how much this means to me." She said to them.

Bootknife walked over to her and gave her a hug. "You are more than welcome. There's nothing that would have prevented us from coming over here."

Bootknife went back to the bed and gave Tommy another hug and then the three of them walked out. None of them spoke a word all the way back to Bootknife's house. They didn't have to say anything because they all knew what each other were thinking. It was the most humbling experience of their life. They all smoked a cigarette together and then went on their way. Bootknife's phone rang as the Killa was pulling out. It was one of the guys at work, looking to see if he would work a swap that night. Bootknife accepted because that meant be would be home a little after 11pm. He never passed up an opportunity to sleep in his own bed at night.

Chapter 6

Bootknife's eight-hour shift was over before he knew it. He had managed to keep himself busy enough where the night flew by. He passed on some information to the third shift guys and walked to his car. He turned the channel selector knob on his pager over to the open selection after he got into his car. He started the engine and took off. Usually in the morning after a third shift, he would hang around for a bit and chat with the guys relieving him. Tonight, however, he wanted to get home and get to bed. While he was at work, there had been two medical calls and an open burn call for Hose Company 1. He wondered if it would be a quiet night. He didn't mind getting up in the middle of the night for calls, but he preferred a full night's sleep was preferred at times.

When Bootknife got home, Vera's car was in the driveway, and he could see a sliver of light coming from under the shade of his bedroom window. After putting his car in the garage, he had one last cigarette for the night and went upstairs. When he got to his room, Vera was sitting up in his bed on her computer.

"Hey there baby," she said, looking up from her laptop.

"What's going on?" asked Bootknife.

"Not much. Just checking some email and stuff. Did you see the pictures Slim put up online tonight?"

"Nope."

"He made a pretty bad ass picture of a patch he wants your brother to make. Check it out."

"Holy shit! That's awesome!"

Slim had taken the IAFF logo and changed the letters on it so they were IALY, International Association of Local Yokels. Under the logo was Local 3103 1/3. It looked great and had already received a ton of comments. The term Local Yokels had become viral, and all the firefighters from Headquarters and Hose Company 1 were calling each other by the newly proclaimed nickname.

"This is great! I bet that ass hole from the newspaper would shit his pants if he realized we had gotten over what he wrote about us," Bootknife said.

Vera looked puzzled. "What are you talking about?"

"Some ass hole wrote to the paper about how pissed off he was that we shut down the Avenue the other day at the apartment fire. You have to read it to understand."

Bootknife pulled up the article online and had Vera read it. Her response was similar to theirs that morning after reading it. After she was done with her response, Bootknife explained to her where the IALY 3103 1/3 came from. After that, she thought the design was pretty damn funny.

Slim had also put up some pictures of him and his girlfriend. Vera still had no idea how Slim had landed her. She was a Pakistani model. She was fit, tan, and beautiful. Vera saw Slim as, well, none of those. Vera was always commenting on the two of them. Whenever she asked Bootknife, "How did Slim get her?" His response would be something along the lines of, "He's a stud horse. You don't see it?" He would laugh and she would continue to ponder how the two ever met.

While Vera finished up checking her messages, Bootknife went into the bathroom and got ready for bed. It had been a long day and he was still thinking about what was to come. He climbed into bed, turned out the light, gave Vera a good night kiss and fell asleep.

It didn't take long for the dreams to start. He was back in Iraq again. This dream was different from the others he had had. He was in his converted refrigeration trailer, finishing up some work. It was approximately midnight and just as he saved his work, he heard an explosion. Then he heard a second, and a third. They grew closer. He ran and grabbed his flak jacket and threw it on over his head. As he reached for his Kevlar helmet, there was a flash and a loud bang, and he was thrown across the container. He was slammed against the side of the container and then he flashed to being in that room again with Bristol. Before he could figure out what had happened, there was a flashover in the room and he was engulfed in flames. He was flailing around burning when he was shaken awake. Vera was saying his name as she tried to wake him.

"What happened?" he gasped.

"You were rolling around saying you were on fire. You must have been dreaming again."

"Huh?"

"You're okay now. You were dreaming."

"Huh? Ah, yeah. I guess I was." He was slowing his breathing by now. He recognized that he was in his own bedroom and that he was safe.

"You okay?" she asked.

"Yeah. Yeah. I'm good. I'm good."

He looked at the clock and saw that it was 3am. He rolled over and shut his eyes again. Vera wrapped her arms around him and fell asleep. The next time Bootknife awoke, it was a little before 8am. The sun was bright, coming in under his shade. The air was already hot and muggy. Vera's legs were stuck to his where their sweaty bare skin touched. He peeled his legs from hers slowly so he wouldn't wake her. It was an unsuccessful attempt though. She woke up just as he swung his legs over the side of his bed.

"What time is it?" She asked, wiping the sleep out of her eyes.

"It's just before eight."

"Where are you going?"

"To the bathroom. I'm going to shower and get moving. I have a feeling our fire streak isn't over."

"Can you just stay in bed with me for a little while longer?"

"Not today. I'm up now."

"Errrr! Okay. Can you do me a favor though, before you get in the shower?"

"Sure. What is it?"

"Can you get me more water, please?" She asked, handing him her water glass.

"Yeah. No prob."

He took the glass and went downstairs to the kitchen. Bootknife ran the water from the sink until it was cold and filled the glass. He walked back upstairs, gave her the glass back, got some clothes pulled out, and went to the shower. When he finished, he walked back to his room still toweling off and found Vera putting on some shorts and a t-shirt.

"Leaving me already?" he asked her.

"Yeah. Wheels sent me a text asking if I wanted to go to the gym. I'm meeting her at school in twenty minutes, so I have to get moving."

"Alright. Well, have fun getting your swell on."

Vera giggled and said, "Thanks. I'll call you later."

Vera gave him a kiss and left. Bootknife finished getting dressed and headed downstairs. He grabbed something to eat really quick, got into his car, and drove to the firehouse. When he pulled in, Slim was already there sitting on the front of Engine 2. Shakes' car was in the parking lot as well. Bootknife parked his car, and when he got out, he yelled over to Slim, "No work today?"

"What's that?" Slim asked, with his hand cupped behind his right ear.

"I said, no work today?"

"Na. My Dad said it was going to be way too hot so he called off work."

"How hot is it supposed to be?"

"Fucking hot, that's what it's gonna be! Upper nineties was what the news was saying this morning."

"Damn! Well, better start drinking water now. Don't want to have to drag your ass out of a fire today because you collapse from heat exhaustion," Bootknife laughed.

"Oh, I already started," said Slim.

Shakes walked out into the bay just as Bootknife and Slim lit a cigarette. He walked over to them, threw his hands in the air and asked, "Didn't want to come ask me if I wanted to smoke with you guys?"

"Nope!" Yelled Slim.

"What's up Bootknife, man? Ready for another fire today, man?" Shakes asked lighting his cigarette.

"Fuckin', A! Hopefully it doesn't come in when it's hot as balls this afternoon."

"What are you talking about? It's already hot as balls right now," Slim said laughing.

The three of them shot the shit for a while out front until Grey arrived. When Grey got out of his truck, he looked excited. He was moving a little faster than normal going in to put his lunch away. He looked over at the Bootknife, Slim, and Shakes and said, "Get ready boys. I could smell something burning coming down the hill, and I thought I saw smoke off in the distance, but I wasn't sure if it was just hazy." He went inside and put his lunch away. Just as he walked through the door into the back of the bay the dispatcher came over the radio. As soon as the dispatcher began speaking, Shakes and Slim ran to their vehicles to grab their gear, and Bootknife ran to his locker.

"Base to Headquarters and Hose Company 1, structure fire at Eight Box Court. I've taken two calls on this already. Neighbors report fire coming out the side of the house." Big'n'Rich, Beamer, Grey, Slim, Shakes, and Bootknife climbed into Engine 5 and took off. Beamer signed them on responding and they were heading through the intersection less than a minute after dispatch. Grey wasn't seeing things. Right as they began climbing the hill, a column of black smoke could be seen off in the distance. Bootknife's cousin L.T. passed them with his blue lights going, heading to the firehouse. Farley followed close behind him. The Tower Ladder signed on a minute later, with Engine 2 signing on right as they pulled up.

"Engine Five on scene, single story wood frame, fire showing from the attic vent on the delta side of the house. House appears to be evacuated at this time. Engine Two, upon your arrival, grab the hydrant two houses before the scene. I believe it is number Four." Beamer put the mic down, grabbed the thermal imager, and met Slim and Grey at the front door. They had a line stretched and were ready to make entry. Shakes and Bootknife were carrying a ladder to the delta side of the house so they could remove the attic vent. They laid the ladder in to the side of the house, just to the left of the attic vent. Bootknife climbed the ladder, and when he was just below the vent he hooked the New York Hook onto the vent screen and waited for the hose team to radio that they gained entry to the attic.

Beamer's voice was heard over the radio a second later, "Five Officer to Five Pump. Charge the line, we are at the attic opening."

That's all Bootknife needed to hear. When he saw the hose whip wildly as the water filled the line, he pulled the hook really hard, ripped the whole vent screen out, and started climbing down the ladder. He didn't want to be anywhere near the vent when they started pushing the fire out. A lot of heat, steam, and debris will fly out as soon as they open the nozzle up.

The Tower and Engine 2 arrived on scene at the same time, coming from different directions on the street. Engine 2 let the Tower go first so they could get up to the house, before they laid into the hydrant and blocked the street. The Tower's crew got off the truck, and Bootknife radioed them to bring a chainsaw so the roof could be opened up. Shakes and Bootknife moved the ladder from the right side of the house, where they first placed it, around to the front. They set it up so the Tower's crew could get up to the roof as soon as they got over there with the saw. L.T.'s crew from Engine 2 took a back-up line, off Engine 5, into the house. He split his crew up and had two standby with the back-up line while the other three began doing a quick search and then checked for signs of extension to any rooms below the fire.

The fire was placed under control after twenty minutes of operating. The crews from Engine 2, Engine 5, and the Tower Ladder remained on scene for another thirty minutes after the fire was extinguished to pick up and ensure there were no hot spots left smoldering. It's really embarrassing if the fire department has to return to the scene of a previous house fire to put another fire out because they missed a pocket of smoldering material.

As soon as everything was repacked on the apparatus, everyone cleared and returned to their respective firehouses. On the way back, Beamer looked back at Grey, Slim, Shakes, and Bootknife and said, "The streak continues!"

"Ya, maaannn!" Shakes replied energetically.

Bootknife grinned and turned his head to look out the window. The sky was hazy off in the distance. The heat and humidity wrapped his body like a blanket. The air blowing in through the window felt nice, but it was time to go with the air conditioner. He rolled up the window, adjusted the vent over his head, and closed his eyes. He tried thinking cool thoughts to assist with cooling down. It wasn't working though.

Chapter 7

Bootknife's alarm went off on his phone, startling him. He laid in place for a minute trying to figure out what was going on. He stretched and rubbed both of his eyes. He looked around and realized that he had fallen asleep on his couch. His living room was dimly lit with the last of the sunlight for the day. He reached over and turned the alarm off, looked at his watch and saw that it was 8pm. Still sitting on the couch, he thought hard about whether he should get up or keep sleeping for a little longer. The smell of sweat and smoke overtook him. "Whoa! I need to shower."

He stretched one last time and slowly got to his feet. He slipped his feet into his sneakers and walked out of the living room. When he passed the calendar hanging on the fridge, he noticed that he had the night off of work. That made him happy because he was exhausted from all the fires. So far, there had been five fires, one a day since Monday. It was Friday night and Bootknife had no plans. Vera was going out of town for the weekend, so he was on his own. When he got to his room, he stripped his clothes off and went to the bathroom. He set his pager on the shelf above the toilet and made sure the volume was all the way up. Looking in the mirror, he noticed he needed to shave. He lathered up his face quickly and ran the blade over his face, one side at a time, until he was finished. Without rinsing his face off, he turned to the shower, moved the curtain to the side a little, and started the water. Once it reached the temperature he was looking for, he jumped in and took a quick, but super thorough, shower.

After finishing in the bathroom, Bootknife went back to his room and had to pick through his laundry baskets to find what he wanted to wear. He wasn't a really stylish guy, but he loved a certain couple pairs of shorts he had that were broken in. Just as he got the belt cinched, he heard his phone ring for a text message. He slipped on a pair of socks and made his way over to his bed. Slim had sent him a message which read:

Titty Bar, 10pm, Be There!

Bootknife had a weakness for strip clubs. He had been known to drop hundreds of dollars in one night. Bootknife was now wide awake and getting excited. It's not very often that Slim is willing to go to a Strip Club. Slim's girlfriend wasn't too fond of nights like this, so to prevent a fight, he would just opt out. Bootknife sent a reply message to find out the details.

Which one? Who's going? Does your girl know about this?

After the message sent, he dropped the phone on his bed and finished getting dressed. By the time he was finished, Slim had replied back.

Top 10. We got a VIP room. There's about 20 or 25 of us going. She's out of town at a photo shoot.

Bootknife sent a short reply back.

See you there!

Bootknife shut the lights off in the house and drove to the bank. He took $500 out of his account and then started driving to Top 10. It took about thirty minutes to get there. When he turned into the parking lot, he recognized ten vehicles, which belonged to various members in town. He parked his car at the far end of the lot and then walked to the front door. Slim was outside on the sidewalk lighting a cigarette as Bootknife walked up.

"You fuckin' made it!" said Slim.

"You thought I'd miss this?" replied Bootknife.

Bootknife lit a cigarette, inhaled deeply, held it for a few seconds then, blew it out. No matter how many strip clubs he'd been to, Bootknife still got a bit of an adrenalin rush. Vera knew he would never cheat on her, so she accepted the fact that he wouldn't turn down a night like tonight.

When Slim and Bootknife finished their cigarettes, Slim wrapped his arm around Bootknife's neck and said, "Ready to party?"

"I was born ready!" replied Bootknife with a huge grin on his face.

Slim took a VIP pass out of his pocket and handed it to Bootknife. As they walked through the front door, they both flashed their passes and were let right in. Inside, the place was packed. All four stages had girls dancing on them. Guys and girls lined all four stages, setting dollar bills in front of them, waiting their turn for a dance. Slim led the way through the crowded rows of tables to the back corner where a large neon sign marked the entrance to the VIP room.

"Who's paying for this? These rooms are expensive," Bootknife asked.

"Don't worry about it. You just enjoy yourself tonight!" Slim replied.

As the two bouncers outside the VIP room doors opened them for Slim and Bootknife, Bootknife could see that Slim hadn't been lying about the number of people attending this party. All eight full time firefighters from town were there. Shakes, Doc, Farley, Bristol, L.T., Killa, Bootknife's younger brother Loo, Patty, and about nine other guys from Headquarters were there as well. When Slim and Bootknife made it into the room, Slim shouted out, "The final guest of honor has arrived!"

Bootknife looked at Slim, with a puzzled look, "What do you mean guest of honor?"

"You'll find out in a second," Slim responded.

Slim climbed the stairs to the DJ booth, picked up the microphone and asked everyone to quiet down for a second. "Thank you to everyone in attendance tonight. This is a special occasion tonight, because we have two real heroes with us tonight. Bristol and Bootknife! They saved that boys life back on Wednesday night, which isn't something we get to actually do around here. Most of the time, the people are out of the structure by the time we get there. Not that night though. If it wasn't for these two guys that boy wouldn't be here today."

Three waitresses were coming around with trays of Soco and Lime shots, passing them out to everyone. Bootknife took one then glared at Slim up in the DJ booth. Once everyone had a shot in hand, Slim continued on with his speech. "So raise your drinks high. To Bristol and Bootknife!"

The entire room of firefighters finished the toast in almost perfect harmony, "Fuck You! Hahahaha"

"Dances and drinks are on the house for Bristol and Bootknife! Everyone drink up and enjoy! Thanks!" Slim set the microphone down and climbed down from the DJ booth. He walked over to Bristol and Bootknife and said, "The owner of this place is the Godfather to the boy you guys saved. This is his way of repaying you guys. Enjoy this shit!"

Bootknife and Bristol looked at each other, grinning like Cheshire Cats. They were floored by the idea that this party was really happening. The three of them turned around as the lights dimmed. The DJ started the music and everyone's attention was on the stage entrance, where two bright lights shined down in front of the curtain. The DJ came over the speakers, "Gentlemen, put your hands together for the entertainers of the evening. Let me introduce to you Candy, Jamie, Jewel, Vixen, Sophie, and Missy." The girls made their way onto the stage and began dancing. About half of the crowd made their way to the stage and started throwing dollar bills down.

Bootknife went up to the bar on the other side of the room and got a beer. He and Slim grabbed a seat in the corner and lit up a cigarette. The girls were getting wild on stage now and everyone in the room was thoroughly enjoying themselves. When the song that was playing ended, the DJ got came over the speakers again. "How's everyone doing?" The crowd in the room erupted with cheers. "Alright! Now, where are the two heroes? Bristol and Bootknife?"

Slim and Grey were standing next to the two and started shouting, "Over here!"

Missy and Jewel came down from the stage and walked up to them. Missy took Bootknife's hand and Jewel took Bristol's hand. They escorted both of them up on stage where Candy and Jamie had set up two chairs, which faced the crowd. The girls told Bristol and Bootknife to sit down and then the DJ started the music again. The six girls split up and they each took turns dancing on them. When Jewel straddled Bootknife, she grabbed the collar of his t-shirt, looked back at the crowd and asked them, "Should I?" She made a tearing motion with her hands. Slim, who was right against the stage, shouted, "Yeeeaaaahhhh!" That's all it took. She ripped the t-shirt in half, right down the middle. Slim started laughing his ass off.

"That was a new shirt!" Bootknife said to Jewel. He couldn't be mad though.

"Aww, sorry sweetie. I guess I'll have to make it up to you with a private dance after we're done up here." Jewel replied with a sly smile on her face.

Bootknife looked at the other five girls and said, "How about you and Missy make it up to me, together?"

Jewel tilted her head back to the right, pretending to think about the suggestion then said quickly, "Okay!"

Missy agreed with the plan. As soon as the performance ended on stage, the two of them hooked an arm through Bootknife's, and off they went to the private dance room. As they passed Slim and Killa, Killa shouted, "Get 'em!"

Slim followed with "See ya in a half hour…or hour! Hahaha."

The party ended at 3am. Everyone stumbled out of the club and went next door to the hotel. They had all drank too much to drive home. The owner of the club had talked to the manager at the hotel earlier in the evening and had reserved the Penthouse for everyone to stay in. The owner of the club told them all before they left, "Only the best, for the bravest!"

Chapter 8

Bootknife woke up to the sound of a door closing. He rolled over to see Candy tiptoeing across the Penthouse with two boxes of coffee in her hands. Not quite sure what was going on, Bootknife sat up and looked around. He was missing his shirt, there were people passed out all over the large room, and Slim was being spooned by Missy. Looking down to the left and right of him, he found Jewel and Sophie. The last thing he could remember was walking over to the hotel, so he decided to ask Candy what happened since she was the only one up. He slowly got to his feet, careful not to wake anyone around him. He stepped over Missy and Slim, and then made his way to the kitchen to see Candy.

"Good Morning!" Candy whispered.

"Morning. You're up early," Bootknife replied.

"Yeah, I'm a light sleeper so I don't sleep for long periods. You want some coffee?"

"That would be great. Thanks." Bootknife's voice was rough from all the cigarettes he smoked that night. His back was sore from sleeping on the floor. Luckily he had a pillow to sleep on because his neck would have been really stiff if he didn't.

"What happened after we left the club this morning?" He looked at his watch to check what time it was. "Wow, its ten a.m. already?"

"Yeah. You guys have been out cold since five."

"Five?"

"Yup. You don't remember the after party?" Candy asked. "You were the life of the party!" she said while winking at him.

"Ummm, can't say that I do remember," he said as he took the cup of coffee from her. "I, uh, didn't embarrass myself did I?"

"Embarrass yourself? Absolutely not! All of the girls kept saying they wanted to party with you all of the time."

"Ah…ok. HHHaha."

"Oh yeah, Slim kept mentioning you had a girlfriend, so the girls behaved themselves…the best they could with you," she giggled. She excused herself then tiptoed down the hallway into the bathroom.

"What the fuck does that mean?" He whispered to himself.

Bootknife heard the shower turn on, and a couple of seconds later the bathroom door opened. Candy popped her head out and asked, "You want one more show to end this wild night?"

Bootknife sat and thought about it. He looked around and saw everyone else was still sleeping. He looked back at Candy and nodded his head. He grabbed his coffee and ran down the hallway. He went through the door way, looking back quick to make sure he didn't wake anyone up, then closed the door behind him.

Twenty minutes later, Bootknife opened the bathroom door and walked out into the hallway. He had no idea what kind of freaky things could be done, by using generic items in the bathroom. The jets in the tub produced the best show though. As he walked back into the kitchen he saw a closet door on the other side of the room open up, and Killa fell out. The loud crashing sound made as he landed on top of the coffee table, breaking all four legs, woke everyone in the suite. Killa let out a loud grown before slowly picking himself up.

Slim started laughing and asked Killa, "What the fuck's wrong with you? You get new legs over night?"

"Fuck you!" Killa replied, checking himself over to make sure he wasn't bleeding anywhere. "Is that coffee I smell?" He looked over in the direction of the kitchen and saw Bootknife sitting at the counter. "Someone's up early. Holy shit! Last night was chaos."

"I can't believe you just broke that table!" Slim said, still laughing. His loud laugh wasn't helping those who were hungover.

It took a couple minutes for most of the guys to get their bearings together enough to stand up and make their way to the kitchen. By then, Candy was out of the bathroom and back in the kitchen pouring coffee for everyone. They were a pretty rough looking crowd when they all came up to take a cup.

Farley looked at Slim and asked, "So, where do you put last night into the epic nights line up? Higher than the GWGs at Bootknife's house? I'm saying they're about even. Too close to call."

Slim thought about it for a minute then said, "I think you're right. Definitely tied with Bootknife's party."

"Anyone know if there were any more fires last night?" Shakes asked.

"Nope, nothing on the pager and no texts. I think it was quiet across town." said Doc.

"Alright, well it's been fun. Thanks for the party all. See ya." Bristol walked out the door followed by everyone shouting, "see ya" to him.

"Well," said Bootknife, "I think I'm going to take off too. Thanks again everyone. See ya at the big one!"

Candy ran after him and got his attention just before he closed the door to the suite. "Bootknife, umm, here's my card with the other girls names written down on the back. Next time you guys have a party, give us a shout."

"Thanks. We will," he replied, giving her a wink as he took the business card.

It was a good thing Bootknife had worn a button down shirt over his t-shirt. It would have been a little embarrassing walking through the hotel lobby shirtless. When he reached his car, he opened the driver's door and threw the torn t-shirt into the passenger seat. The inside of the car was sweltering since it was already almost 90 degrees out, and the car hadn't been parked in the shade. Bootknife reached over to the console and shut off the air conditioner since it was blowing nothing but hot air in his face. He rolled all four windows down, put it in drive, and took off. It looked like most of the guys were exiting the front of the hotel as he drove by.

He had a feeling that the fire streak wasn't over yet, so he moved right along once he hit the highway. When he hit the town line, Headquarters got dispatched for a medical call. When he was pulling into his driveway, the East Side got dispatched for an open burn complaint. He decided to leave his car outside in the driveway, and ran upstairs to shower and change. He had to get the smell of old booze off of himself. When he was done showering and changing, he grabbed a pile of his dirty clothes and brought it down to the basement to do a load of laundry. As he popped the knob out to start the washer, the tones hit and he was off.

Chapter 9

After placing his helmet in the top shelf of his locker, hanging his bunker coat up, and cramming his bunker pants into the bottom of the locker, Bootknife pulled his phone from his pocket to see if he missed any phone calls. There was a text message from Vera saying she wasn't getting back into town until late on Sunday, so she would just go back to her house that night. He sent a quick reply to let her know he got the message, went to sign in, and then walked out front of the firehouse to have a cigarette. Shakes and Killa were standing in front of Engine 5 when Bootknife got outside.

"Smoke?" Bootknife asked Shakes and Killa.

"Yeah man!" they both said.

"Haven't had a wreck like that in a while. I'm glad I stopped by here on my way home. I wouldn't have made the truck if I didn't," Killa said, taking a drag on his cigarette.

"Yeah, that wasn't a bad wreck. I'm still waiting for my chance to be on a tool though. I'm always in the back seat, which sucks sometimes." Bootknife said in return.

Since Bootknife was an EMT, he usually ends up taking patient care and never gets to use the spreaders or cutters at a real accident scene. Usually, the only time he gets his hands on the tools is at the annual extrication drill and the scared straight drill at the high school.

"Whoa, look who's a day late and a dollar short!" said Bootknife, as he watched Slim pull into the driveway. "Where were you? You missed the wreck!"

"I had to go back to Top Ten because I lost my pager," Slim said laughing.

"What an idiot!" Shakes said, laughing harder than Slim.

"Whatever. What did you guys have?" Slim asked, as he too lit a cigarette.

"Guy got T-Boned when he ran the light on the avenue, just passed the high school. Had to pop the front and back doors on the driver side. Rear passenger had no seatbelt on and was pretty banged up. The driver of the other car wasn't hurt, surprisingly." Killa said.

The four of them stood there and talked about the wreck for twenty minutes. It was like a mini critique, talking about what went well and what went not so well. Slims phone rang, taking him away from the conversation for a couple minutes. When he returned he told Bootknife that their friend Big Red wanted to hangout and was on his way down. Big Red had been a friend of Bootknife and Slim since middle school. He was built like Slim, but he had fire red hair and a beard. Big Red had just graduated college with a degree in fire science and had moved back to town in early May. Slim and Bootknife had been pushing him to join the fire department, but he still hadn't filled out an application.

Big Red pulled into the firehouse parking lot a few minutes after he had gotten off the phone with Slim. He climbed out of his car and strolled up to where everyone was still standing. "Bootknife, what's going on buddy?"

"Ahhh, hangin' in there man. You?"

"I'm doing pretty good. I saw you had a couple fires this week. After that ass hole had written that letter to the paper, they've had an article about you guys every day. How many fires have you guys had so far?"

"Five since Monday. Still waiting for today's to come."

"Oh yeah? No fire today yet?"

"Nope. We had to cut a couple people out of a car just a little while ago, but no fire. Hopefully the streak hasn't ended yet!"

"I bet. How many of those fires have you made?"

"I've made all of them."

"Slim told me you and Bristol got a grab the other day as well. Congrats man!"

"Yeah, thanks. We almost burnt up too, but no biggy," Bootknife chuckled a little. "Speaking of which, I think this may be him pulling in right now."

Everyone looked to the end of the driveway and saw a dark-blue minivan pulling into the lot. A shadow of a face and waving hand could be seen through the tinted rear window. The girl who was driving the van didn't look familiar though. She got out of the driver seat, walked around to the passenger side of the van and opened the slider door. Around the back of the van came a young boy running like crazy waving his hand at all the guys in front of the firehouse. It was the boy Bootknife had saved, Tommy. He still had the hospital bracelet on his wrist. He ran up to Bootknife and gave him a big hug.

"Hey there Bootknife!" Tommy said excitedly. "The doctors let me out of the hospital. They said I have to take it easy for a little while, but they said it would be alright to go to the firehouse on my way home!"

"Excellent buddy!" Bootknife replied. "Do you want to see the rigs? You can even drive if you want."

Tommy's eyes lit up and were the size of saucers. "Can I?" he asked.

"Of course! Killa's going to help me. Isn't that right Killa?"

"Yup." said Killa.

Just before they walked into the bay, the girl who was driving came up to the group. She introduced herself as Tommy's sister. She was a pretty, young, blond who was no older than 20. While Killa and Bootknife were showing them the apparatus, they found out that she had been out with friends the night of the fire. They toured the apparatus, and then they went inside the firehouse to look at all of the pictures. They were there for about 30 minutes before they had to leave so they could meet the rest of their family next door for dinner. Bootknife gave Tommy a plastic fire helmet and told him to come by anytime to visit. Tommy thanked him and Killa, and then he and his sister left.

Bootknife and Killa joined Slim and Big Red out front again. Shakes had just left. Bootknife lit a cigarette then said, "Wow, that girl was pretty hot."

Big Red snapped his head to the left and looked at Bootknife with an intense stare, "Pretty hot?! Pretty hot?! She was a smoke show! Did you see her ass?"

Slim started laughing, "Big Red has a point. She was fucking hot."

"Okay, Okay! She was hot!" Bootknife confessed.

"Thank you!" said Big Red.

Bootknife flicked the cherry off the end of his cigarette and walked over to the cigarette bin. He dropped it in through the hole as dispatch came over the radio, "Hose Company One and Headquarters, respond to Thirty-Six Clover Street for a structure fire. Occupants are evacuating at this time. We've taken two calls on this already."

Big Red was all excited. Clover Street was the street where the Old Firehouse was on the corner. "Does anyone have a camera? I'm gonna go buff this job!"

Slim grabbed his camera from his truck and tossed it to Big Red as he ran by to get in his car. Big Deve came flying into the parking lot just as Big Red was pulling out. A black column of smoke could be seen coming from the hill visible from the front of the firehouse. "Let's go Big Deve!" yelled Slim.

"Start Engine Five for me while I get my gear on," replied Big Deve.

Killa opened the driver door, reached into the cab and started the engine. Big Deve came running inside as Killa climbed into the back of the engine with Bootknife. As Big Deve was pulling the Engine out of the bay, Shakes pulled into a parking spot and started running for his locker. Big Deve stopped just outside of the firehouse and waited for Shakes to jump in. When Slim heard the back door slam shut, he turned around and yelled, "All set back there?"

"Yeah maaannnn! Hit it!" replied Killa.

Big Deve pulled the Engine out onto the street and started heading towards the intersection. As they passed the restaurant where the boy's family was eating, Bootknife saw the Tommy on the patio waving. He stuck his hand out the window and threw him a quick wave back as he finished getting his arms through the straps of the air pack. He tugged on the tightening straps and then pulled the release cord. A few seconds later, they were pulling up to the driveway of 36 Clover Street. Bootknife looked to the left and saw fire coming out of a second floor window. Bootknife slid forward on the seat until his airpack popped out of the holder, and then he stood up and stepped off the rig.

The homeowner ran up to Killa and Bootknife as they began stretching a 1-3/4 inch hose line, "Save my house! Please!"

Killa tried to reassure him, "We're going to do our best. Is there anyone in the house?"

"No! Everyone is out. They're next door at the neighbors. Please save my house! Please!"

"Slim, everyone's out of the house!"

"Roger that!" Slim said and then reported the message over the radio to dispatch.

The homeowner had left the front door open, and there was a little bit of smoke curling out from the top of the door. When Killa and Bootknife got to the top step, before entering the house, they had Big Deve charge the line. While they waited for water, they put on their masks and got ready to move in. The line kicked forward a couple feet as the water filled the hose. Killa opened the nozzle and bled the air out of it. After flowing water for a couple seconds, he closed the bale, and they moved through the door. The stairs were to the right as they came through the door. The smoke was thick at the top of the landing, but there wasn't any fire that they could see.

When Killa and Bootknife reached the top of the stairs, they could feel the heat coming down the hallway. Looking for a glow in the distance, they pushed through the increasing heat in search of the fire room. They could hear a faint crackle of fire and knew they were close. They crawled a couple feet further, and then Killa shouted back to Bootknife, "I got a glow close to the ceiling in front of me."

The glow grew more and more defined, until the heat was almost unbearable. Killa opened the bale and started flowing water, directing it toward the glow. The glow began to push back, so they advanced forward. The homeowner had closed the door to the hallway, which was smart because it had kept the fire from spreading down the length of the hallway. The top of the door had just burned away, but Killa and Bootknife had gotten there just in time. They pushed the door open to find a well-involved room. Heat poured out trying to beat them down, but the heat was unsuccessful. Killa and Bootknife dug in hard and stood their ground as they directed the water into the room. After hitting it hard for a couple minutes, it finally appeared that they had knocked the fire down.

Water damage was kept minimal in the room below the fire room, thanks to the quick thinking of Slim and Shakes. After making sure the hose line was flaked out properly to prevent kinks, they went back to the Engine and grabbed a couple tarps. They put the tarps over what items they could, then joined Killa and Bootknife upstairs around the time the fire was put out. Slim crawled up the hose to where Killa and Bootknife were and asked, "How's it looking?"

"Fire's out. We're going to keep wetting things down until the smoke clears," replied Bootknife.

As the smoke began to clear, the Chief ordered Engine 5's crew out of the house. He sent in fresh crews to finish hitting hotspots and mop up. Killa and Bootknife left the hose line in place in the fire room, so it could be used by the overhaul crew if needed. They then made their way downstairs. When they exited the front of the house, Bootknife took his helmet off, pulled his flash hood back, and removed his mask. When he reached the lawn, he set his helmet down in the grass and wiped the sweat from his head and face with his gloved hand. He glanced back over his shoulder to see how much damage had been done. Surprisingly, most of the damage appeared to have been only inside of the fire room. Around the window, where the fire was showing on arrival, the siding was burned and melted, and there was a smoke stain on the roof above. But other than that, they had made a good, quick knock down.

Chapter 10

Bootknife hardly had a chance to step off the Engine when Big Red came running up to him with Slim's camera in his hand. "You have to see these photos! I got some great shots of you guys in action!" said Big Red excitedly. "I think you can see the devil's face in one of them."

"Nice! We'll put them onto the computer as soon as I get my gear off and we get the rig back in service," said Bootknife.

Bootknife walked back to his locker, hung up his coat, and put his helmet in the top cubby. Then he walked back to the Engine to pull the equipment they used off and rinse it down. The used air bottles were put into the back of Farley's pickup so they could be refilled at Headquarters. Then everyone pitched in to spread the salvage tarps out in front of the bays to hose them down. Once everything had been cleaned and put back, Bootknife took his bunker pants off and put them in his locker. He picked up his sneakers and headed to the office. His socks were soaked so he wanted to let them dry out a little before putting his shoes on.

Slim and Big Red were on the computer working on uploading the pictures when Bootknife walked in. Shakes and Killa came in a moment later, excited to see how the pictures came out. They had just finished loading when the Chief came in. "What do we have here?"

"Big Red took some pictures of us in action up there," replied Slim.

"Nice!" said the Chief as he positioned himself behind everyone who was already crowded around the computer.

"What's going on in here?" asked Doc as he walked into the office. He was curious why there were so many people huddled around the computer.

"Someone want to put a sign up outside the door so we don't have to keep answering the same question?" said Slim laughing.

"Eat shit Slim," said Doc in response to Slim's joke. "I didn't know what was happening in here."

"Whoa! Easy Doc. Don't get your panties in a bunch!" Slim said, laughing even harder this time.

Big Red opened the photo folder and clicked on the view slide show option. The first photo popped up, and was of Killa and Bootknife stretching the hose line up the front yard. He kept clicking to advance to the next picture. About four or five pictures in Big Red broke the silence, "The next picture is the one with the devil in it." When he clicked on that picture he made it a full screen view, and pointing to the top right corner said, "See it?"

"Holy shit!" said Shakes. "That's crazy! Hahaha."

Everyone leaned in closer to look at the picture. Sure enough, in the middle of the flames blowing out of the window was a dark section that looked like a crazy shaped head with a long pointed chin. There were two bright spots that looked like eyes, another bright spot resembling a pointy nose, and a spot that looked like a mouth that was slightly opened. Just below and to the left of that window was Bootknife and Killa in the doorway with the charged line. Bootknife was looking up and right, at the stairs, but the stairs weren't visible in the picture so it looked like he was staring right at that devilish face.

"I want that picture!" Bootknife said. "I want an eight-by-ten of that picture! That thing is going up on my wall at home."

"Same here!" Said Killa.

The Chief looked at Slim and said, "I think we need to put this picture up on the wall down here, in the other room. So, get three copies made!"

After they finished going through the rest of the photos, Killa and Shakes left. Bootknife, Slim, and Big Red went out front and had a cigarette before Big Red drove them to pharmacy up the street to get the photos developed. When they got back to the firehouse, Bootknife took his copies and went home to shower.

While Bootknife was grabbing some clothes from his dresser, his phone started ringing. He looked at the caller ID and saw that it was Slim. "Hello?"

"What are you doing?"

"Just getting dressed, what's up?"

"Big Red was wondering if you wanted to grab some food. Buffalo Chicken Pizza?"

"Ah, sure. Yeah, I'll go in on that. Where are we meeting?"

"Firehouse. Fifteen minutes."

"Roggggeeeerrrr! See ya then."

Bootknife hung up and finished getting dressed. He went downstairs and put the photos from the fire into the frames he bought. As soon as he finished he went downstairs, got in his car and started making his way to the firehouse. Along the way, he stopped at the gas station to grab a bottle of vitamin water and a pack of cigarettes. Slim was out front smoking with Big Red when Bootknife pulled into the parking lot. "You get the pizza yet?" he asked, walking up to them.

"Yeah. Its inside," answered Slim.

"Finish those up so we can eat it before it gets cold," said Bootknife, walking towards the front door.

The three of them walked inside and got some paper plates out of the back room before eating. When Bootknife had finished eating, he sat back in his chair and let the digestion process begin. Slim let out a loud fart, which started everyone laughing. "Welcome to the Hose!" he said, in tears.

In the middle of the laughter, dispatch came over the radio, "Hose Company One, medical call for the party not breathing, unknown pulse…" Slim and Bootknife got up and ran out to the medical truck. Doc must have pulled into the parking lot right as the dispatch was coming over, because he came out of nowhere, jumping into the back of the truck. Slim pulled out of the bay slowly, as he didn't want to rip the exhaust vent tube out of the ceiling, and floored it as soon as the tube was free of the truck. Slim pulled onto the street of the emergency, and they could see two police cars on scene already. The dispatcher came over the radio before they pulled up to the house, "Base to Medic Sixteen?"

Bootknife picked up the mic and answered, "Sixteen's on scene, go ahead base."

"Sixteen, be advised, my officers on scene report no medical emergency. The party was just sleeping."

"Ten-four! We're out with PD right now."

After Bootknife talked to the police officer he called back to dispatch, "Base from sixteen, cancel the assignment. Confirmed person sleeping."

"Roger!" replied the dispatcher, and then he called the other responding units to cancel them.

Doc leaned forward, in between the front two seats, and said jokingly, "Sounds like someone didn't want to talk to his wife anymore, so he played dead."

"Hahaha, I think you're right," said Bootknife.

There weren't many people at the firehouse when they got back. Bootknife was starting to get tired, so after he signed in, he said farewell to Big Red and Slim and went home. As soon as he got home, he went right upstairs to his room, and fell face first onto his bed. It didn't take long at all for him to fall asleep. As soon as he closed his eyes, he was out cold.

Bootknife woke up when he heard his phone ringing. When he had gotten into bed, it was dark, but there was still a little light because the sun had just gone down. Now, it was completely dark. He looked at his clock and saw that it was just after midnight. "Who's calling me at this time of night?" he mumbled. When he looked at the caller ID, he saw that it was Vera. "Hey baby," he said in a rough, sleepy voice.

"Hey there sesy man!" she replied. "What are you doing?"

By the way Vera was speaking, Bootknife knew that she had been drinking. "I was asleep. Have you been drinking?"

"Oh, sorry for waking you," she said lowering her voice to almost a whisper, "I just wanted to call and say, good night. Sorry for bothering you."

"Night, Night. I'll call you in the morning," said Bootknife starting to fall back asleep.

"Okee-dokee."

Vera hung up the phone, leaving Bootknife with the feeling that she was mad at him for cutting their conversation short. Bootknife wasn't too worried about it though because he knew she probably wouldn't remember even talking to him by morning. He kicked off his sneakers, took his pager off his belt and put it on the nightstand. The room was pretty hot, so he crawled to the other side of his bed and turned on the fan. After he crawled back to his side of the bed, he grabbed his phone and sent a text message to Vera. I hope you don't think I'm mad. I miss you and hope you're having fun! Kisses and talk to you tomorrow! He set the phone down on the nightstand, laid his head on his pillow, and closed his eyes. It took less than a minute for him to fall back to sleep.

Chapter 11

BEEEEEEEEEEEP! Bootknife sprang out of bed and began getting dressed. "Base to Hose Company One and Headquarters, structure fire, Twenty River Street. I've taken multiple calls on this. Time, six-forty."

Bootknife was pulling out of his garage as the dispatcher was finishing the dispatch. The adrenaline was flowing as he rushed to the firehouse. Just before turning into the firehouse parking lot Bootknife looked in his rearview mirror and saw Doc and Domer about to come through the intersection. Big Deve was in front of him, just coming past the gazebo. Bootknife parked his car quickly and began running to the front door to unlock it. Just before he got to the building, he saw Slim flying down between the firehouse and the restaurant. Bootknife pulled his bunker pants out of his locker, kicked his shoes to the side, and stepped into his boots. He pulled up his bunker pants and put his arms through his suspenders. Doc came running up to his locker as Bootknife was pulling his helmet out of the cubby and pulling his bunker coat off the hook.

Bootknife ran down to the garage door and opened it so Big Deve, Domer, and Slim could get in. Bootknife put his coat on, finished buckling his bunker pants and harness, and then climbed into the back of Engine 5. Domer and Doc climbed in behind him, and Slim climbed into the officer's seat. Big Deve threw his gear into the rig and started it up. Killa was pulling in as Big Deve was releasing the parking brake. Slim told Big Deve to pull down to Killa and grab him.

Killa had managed to get his bunker pants on by the time Big Deve pulled up behind his truck. He pulled his coat and helmet out of the back of his truck and climbed into the back of the Engine with Domer, Doc, and Bootknife.

"Everybody ready?" Big Deve asked.

"Yeah!" Bootknife hollered up to him as he was tightening the air pack straps down. Big Deve swung the truck to the right then back to the left, out onto the street. As they took the left out of the driveway, Bootknife looked out the right side of the rig and saw five more cars with blue lights flashing pulling down the street, trying to get to the firehouse.

Slim laid on the air horns and pegged the pedal for the federal siren. The wail of the siren and the blasting air horns echoed in the intersection as Big Deve made a tight left turn to go over the bridge. A thick black column of smoke could be seen just on the other side of the river. Slim turned around and yelled, "We got a job!"

Everyone in the back moved their heads so they could see what Slim was talking about. Bootknife leaned forward and hit Killa's leg to get his attention. "You fucking ready for this shit, you local yokel?" he yelled over the sound of the siren and air horns.

"Fuckin', A! You crazy mothafucka!" Killa said laughing.

Domer had his serious face on as Big Deve maneuvered the left turn onto River Street. This was the first fire this week that Domer made the first rig. Bootknife saw his expression and asked him, "You okay?" Domer just nodded his head.

The house was down a long narrow driveway. Flames could be seen through the trees that covered the front of the property. Slim got on the radio, calling dispatch, "Engine Five's on scene. Two story wood frame, fire showing from the first and second floors on the right half of the alpha side. Second engine in, hit the hydrant at the end of the driveway and lay in." Slim took the portable out of the charger next to him and put it in his pocket. He looked at Big Deve and yelled to him, "Give me foam!" Slim pulled the thermal imager out of the holder and stepped down from the rig.

Doc and Domer were stretching the 2-1/2 inch crosslay when the homeowner ran up to them screaming hysterically, "My two boys are upstairs! Save them! Please save them! At the top of the stairs, go to the right and they're in the first room on the left!"

Slim got on the radio and called the dispatcher, "Engine 5 to base, be advised we have two parties trapped on the second floor!" As soon as he released the mic, he pointed at Bootknife and Killa, who were working on pulling a 1-3/4" crosslay, and said, "Take that line with you to the second floor and find those kids!" Slim looked at Doc and Domer and told them that they were with him and to start hitting the fire on the first floor.

Bootknife pulled the hose off the truck and moved quickly to the front door, flaking it out as he went. Killa grabbed a set of irons and met him at the front door. Doc, Domer, and Slim moved in through the front door and started attacking the intense flames on the first floor. Bootknife and Killa put on their masks quicker than they had ever done before. Big Deve charged their hose line, Bootknife bled the air out, closed the bale, and they moved in.

The staircase was like a chimney. The heat from the fire on the first floor pushed them down on the steps. They moved as fast as they could up the stairs so they wouldn't be beat up too badly by the heat. About half way up the stairs, everything went pitch black due to the amount of thick black smoke that was trapped on the second floor. The smoke had nowhere to go but down, since there was no ventilation yet. Bootknife and Killa reached the second floor landing and could see the glow of the fire raging at the end of the hallway. There was a similar glow that was hugging the right side of the hallway as well, which was the fire in the two rooms on the front side of the house.

The heat was really intense now. The heat had Killa and Bootknife pinned to the floor. They needed ventilation soon. Bootknife heard the

Chief arrive on scene along with Engine 2. The Chief talked to Big Deve, got an update of who was working, and assumed command. Engine 2 dropped Saxmo off at the hydrant and started laying the supply line down the driveway. Saxmo had the hydrant opened up and was in the process of hooking the hose up to it when Engine 2 stopped behind Engine 5. Big Deve was at the back of Engine 5, and as soon as Engine 2 stopped, he grabbed the pre-connected supply line on the front bumper and hooked it into the intake valve on Engine 5. He needed water fast because Engine 5 only had a quarter of a tank left.

Bootknife keyed up the radio mic, "Engine Five Search to Command?"

"Command's on."

"Command, we need the roof opened up fast. The heat is intense on the second floor. Visibility is zero!"

"Roger that. Engine Two, ladder the roof and start venting it!"

Loo was the officer on Engine 2, rogering up on the Chief's order. He told Shakes and L.T. to handle ventilation. Right after he finished giving them their assignment he heard Bootknife come over the radio again. "Five Search to Command?"

"Command's on."

"Command, we need a ladder to the two windows closed to the delta corner of the house on the charlie side. Vics are reported to be in one of those rooms."

"Roger. Two, take the remainder of your crew and ladder the back of the house."

"Two copies." Loo, Smeagle, and Meagle grabbed two ladders and moved quickly to the back of the house. They set the ladders up, placing the tip of the ladder under the windowsills. By the time this was completed, L.T. and Shakes were starting to cut the vent hole in the roof.

While the ladders were being set up and the ventilation started, Bootknife and Killa had been working on knocking the fire at the end of the hallway down enough so they could reach the first room. When they got to the door, Bootknife kept the hose stream directed down the hallway to provide protection while Killa made entry and conducted a search of the room. Bootknife could feel the change in temperature when L.T. and Shakes had finished the vent hole. The temperature went down drastically, although it was still extremely hot. By this point, Bootknife was feeling like he had been baked twice over. Every breath of air coming into his mask was hot, and his arms and shoulders felt like they had a really bad sunburn on them. As he looked around checking the conditions above and behind him, he could see a glow coming from overhead. The fire in the fire room on the right was now coming out of the door and burning across the ceiling. He turned the nozzle and directed the foam into the room.

"Bootknife, I found the two vics. Have them break the second window in!" Killa shouted to him.

Bootknife waited for the radio traffic to stop, then keyed up the mic, "Five Search to Command! We have the two vics. Need the second window in from the Charlie-Delta corner broken. We're gonna hand them out to Two's crew in the back."

Command acknowledged Bootknife's transmission, along with Loo acknowledging it too. Bootknife heard breaking glass a second later, as Meagle cleared all the glass from the window frame. Killa started dragging the first victim and yelled out to Bootknife, "I need a hand with the second vic!"

"Roger, on my way!" Bootknife said, closing the bale and entered the room. He brought the hose with him so they had it in case something went wrong. With the window broken out, smoke was venting through it allowing Bootknife to barely make out the outline of Killa dragging the first victim from the bed. Bootknife crawled over to where they were. Reaching up on the second bed, Bootknife could feel the second victim's limp body. Grabbing a hold of the boys arm, he pulled him to the edge of the bed. He then used both hands to get the boy to the floor. As he dragged the boy towards the window, he keyed up the radio mic and said, "Command from Five Search, we need another crew with a line up here on the second floor!"

"Roger Five Search, Engine Six is sending a crew up right now."

When Bootknife got his victim to the window, Killa had just handed the first victim out to Meagle. As soon as she reached the bottom, Loo climbed up to grab the second victim. Killa helped Bootknife lift the boy up into the window and they handed him out to Loo on the ladder. As soon as the second victim was out of the house, Bootknife keyed up the hand mic and reported to the Chief that both victims had been removed from the structure. Bootknife and Killa crawled back to the beds where the hose was left, grabbed it, and started to crawl towards the door. The heat had suddenly increased in the room. Flames could be seen coming through the door and had engulfed over half of the ceiling in the room. Killa opened the bale in the attempt to extinguish the fire, but the fire had burned through the hose. The length of hose burning up, burst and no water came out of the nozzle. The front half of the room was completely engulfed now. Killa and Bootknife were burning up from the extreme heat. Killa dropped the nozzle and they both began crawling towards the window. They were about three feet from the window when they heard a loud CRRRAAACCCCKKK! The ceiling had burned through, from a fire raging in the cockloft, and collapsed in on top of them. They were knocked unconscious and now trapped under the heavy weight of the plaster ceiling and wood joists.

Chapter 12

Bootknife regained consciousness a couple minutes later. His mask had been twisted off his face and his right hand was pinned under his body, luckily though the radio mic was in his hand. He couldn't feel his left arm and both of his legs were completely numb. He tried to move but couldn't. He was completely pinned. The radio was screaming with chatter. He heard a Mayday coming from someone on the first floor reporting a partial collapse which had trapped Slim, as soon as that Mayday was finished, Engine 6 tried to get a Mayday transmission through to report the collapse on the second floor with a hose line coming out from under the debris. As soon as there was a break in radio traffic, Bootknife tried to transmit a Mayday, "May… Mayday, May…"His thumb slipped off the key. When he didn't hear a squelch he knew there was something wrong with his radio. It had been smashed when the collapse happened, and the Maydays he heard were coming from the radios that Engine 6's crews had. In a weak whisper he tried calling out for Killa. There was no response.

"Five Search! Are you in there?" yelled Patty, trying to choke back tears. He was with the second crew, from Engine 6, who went to the second floor with a handline. They got up there right after the collapse. "Can you hear me? Five Search?" The only sound Patty could hear from the room was the high-pitched wail of two pass-alarms could be heard from under the rubble.

Bootknife tried to gather enough strength to yell back, but barely got a whisper out. "In…In, We're…In here." It wasn't loud enough for Patty to hear him. He started to feel light headed and dizzy. He started to feel really tired. He took one more shallow breath. Vera's face flashed in front of him, and then he gave up. He closed his eyes and faded off into darkness.

The first crew from Engine 6 was battling the last of the flames in the room at the end of the hallway when they felt the floor start to sag. "The floor's gonna give. Get the fuck out!" yelled the nozzleman. They dropped the line where it was and began crawling as fast as possible out towards the stairs. They used the hose to lead them in the right direction. When they reached Patty's crew, they had to forcefully push them back to the stairs. "Patty, we have to get out, the second floor isn't stable anymore!"

Patty tried to crawl over the top of the guys coming down the hall so he could get back to the room where Bootknife and Killa were. "We've got firefighters trapped in there!"

The Chief was calling over the radio by then, calling for an evacuation of the building. Big Deve and Sly, the driver of Engine 2, were blowing the air horns. The Chief from Headquarters ran to the top of the stairs and saw the two hose teams trying to get Patty to the stairs. "Hurry up!" he yelled at them. He reached out and grabbed the back of Patty's pack and pulled him backwards. Three people grabbed Patty, picked him up and hauled him down the stairs and out of the building. When they got him out, they had to hold him to the ground and calm him down. The Headquarters' Chief looked him in the eye and said, "Patty, look at me! Look at me and listen! We have three firefighters trapped already and the house is not stable. We can't afford to lose anymore firefighters!" By this point he was even choking back tears. He knew all three of the guys who were trapped. "There's nothing we can do right now!"

The Chief got on the radio, "Command to all units, I need an accountability report!"

"Engine Five, missing three!...Engine Two, all accounted for!...Engine Six, accounted for!...Tower's accounted for!...Rescue Fifteen's accounted for!"

"Engine Five from command, who are the firefighters missing and where were they operating?"

"Command, we're missing Bootknife and Killa who were on the second floor, and Slim who was on the first!" reported Doc.

"Command copies! RIT, start working on getting Slim out. Watch the stability of the building. Tower, send your crew to the second floor and work on getting Killa and Bootknife. If conditions aren't stable enough, back out!"

"RIT copies!...The Tower copies!"

"Command to dispatch, I need three more ambulances to the scene. Get me an Engine and Ladder from Avon to the scene. Also, get me one Engine from the East Side to cover Headquarters."

Dispatch acknowledged the Chief's message and dispatched accordingly. The RIT crew from Rescue 15 entered the house through the front door, sounding the floor in front of them to ensure it was stable. They watched the ceiling and walls to see if there were any signs of further collapse. Things looked good so they kept moving forward. When they reached the room where Slim was trapped, they could see his boot sticking out of the pile of debris. They could hear his pass-alarm going off as well, muffled though due to the debris on top of him.

"Slim, we're here for you bro! We're gonna get you out of here! Hang in there!" yelled Bristol.

The fire had been extinguished prior to the collapse, with the exception of a few hot spots. The RIT crew went right to work removing debris from Slim. One firefighter was assigned the task of monitoring the structural conditions and to hit the hot spots while they worked on clearing away the chunks of ceiling and broken wood joists that covered Slim. The RIT crew worked fast but carefully. One wrong move and Slim could be killed. The pieces of debris were light enough for two firefighters to lift them and move to the side. When they finally reach the bottom of the pile, Slim was unresponsive. His mask was still on his face, however, it was shattered and the air regulator had been torn off the front of it. Slim's bunker gear was torn in multiple spots, and his helmet was cracked in three places. He had blood all over his face and coming out of his ears. His right leg appeared to be broken below the knee and he didn't appear to be breathing.

Bristol removed his glove and checked for a carotid pulse. "He still has a pulse!" he yelled. "We need to get him out of here fast! His pulse is there, but weak."

The RIT crew carefully lifted Slim and Bristol slid the stokes-basket under him. They set Slim down in it, and four of them grabbed a corner. They moved as fast as they could out of the house. On their way out Bristol called the Chief over the radio to notify them Slim was on his way out, and to make sure EMS was on standby.

While the RIT crew was working on getting Slim pulled out, the Tower's crew, plus Loo and L.T., went to the second floor to assess the situation. When they reached the top of the stairs, the heat was starting to build up again in the hallway, due to the fire still burning in the room at the end of the hallway. Loo and L.T. grabbed the hose line Patty had been on, and began attacking the fire from about halfway down the hallway. They didn't want to go any further than that due to the floor being unstable in the room and in the hallway right outside the room. They knew they weren't going to be able to completely extinguish the fire, but they were going to protect the Tower's crew while they worked to get Killa and Bootknife out. They prayed that they were both still alive.

O'Queef, the Lieutenant in charge of the Tower's crew, kneeled in the doorway to the bedroom that Killa and Bootknife were in and looked at the section of ceiling and roof that had collapsed. Most of the pieces were rather large, but most looked like they could be removed by hand. "Form a chain from the doorway, down the stairs, and start passing the debris down the line as it's removed!" he told his crew. He thought to himself, more bodies are going to be needed to make this work. Just then, he heard Bristol give the report that Slim was being removed from the house. O'Queef called over the radio as soon as Bristol's message had been received, "Tower to Command."

"Command on."

"Chief, we're going to need more bodies to get this debris removed."

"Roger, I have two fresh crews from Avon arriving now. They will be inside in a second. Where do you want them?"

"Have them come to the stairs to the second floor and join my crew."

"Roger!"

O'Queef and another firefighter from his crew started pulling chunks of debris from the room and passing them down the chain. It felt like they weren't moving fast enough. It was slow, but after they got the first foot and a half cleared out, things started to move faster. The pieces being moved became bigger as they got farther into the room. O'Queef could see a large slab closer to the window that wasn't going to be able to be moved by hand. He reached for his radio, "Tower to Command."

"Go Tower."

"Command, we are going to need two sets of airbags and cribbing up here. There is a large slab of ceiling we probably won't be able to move by hand."

"Copy. RIT will be on their way in, in a second."

"Keep working guys! We're making a lot of progress!" O'Queef said trying to keep the men encouraged. Work was halted momentarily when the RIT crew came in with the airbags and cribbing. They got there just in time, because the Tower crew had almost reached the large slab. The last couple pieces able to be moved by hand were being passed out of the room when a noise came from under the slab.

"Everyone shut up!" O'Queef yelled.

The noise came again. It was a quiet moan. It was barely audible, but it was there. O'Queef got his face as low to the floor and shouted, "Can't you hear me? Bootknife, Killa, can you hear me?"

"Mayday, Mayday, Mayday! Firefighters down, second floor near the Charlie wall. This is Engine … Engine … Eng …" the voice died out. O'Queef was barely able to hear the Mayday being called. Nothing came over the radio, so he figured whoever was trying to give the Mayday call didn't know their radio was broken.

"Time to move gents! We have at least one survivor under there!" O'Queef said as his crew was placing the airbags under the slab. It wasn't easy getting them in place. Two firefighters had to use halogen bars to lift the slab up enough to slide the bags under each side. The bags were attached to the air bottles, which were used to inflate the bags. A couple firefighters with cribbing were in position to place the pieces of wood under the slab after the airbags were inflated.

"Everyone ready? Start lifting. Lift both sides evenly." O'Queef instructed. After the bags had lifted the slab about four inches, O'Queef ordered them to stop. Box cribbing was started with four pieces of 2x4 inch wood. This was done on either side of each bag so incase a bag failed, the slab would rest on the cribbing, preventing further injury to Killa and Bootknife. After the cribbing was in place, O'Queef took his hand-light and shined it under the slab. When he peered into the void, he could see three boots. The boot closest to the wall was ever so slightly moving. "I can see them. One of them is still moving! Keep inflating both bags. Keep cribbing as we lift."

When the airbags had reached their max inflation, the firefighters who were cribbing finished cribbing the slab. They had about two feet of clearance now. Two New York Hooks were used to hook the bottom of Bootknife's airpack frame and drag him out from under the slab. He was face down, blood stained both legs of his bunker pants, his left arm was like a limp noodle, and his helmet was in pieces, barely being held together by the wire frame. His mask was completely shattered and twisted halfway off his face, which was bruised, swollen, and bloody. O'Queef checked for a pulse. He felt nothing. But right before he removed his fingers from Bootknife's carotid, he thought he felt a slight beat. He repositioned his fingers and checked again. Yes, a faint pulse. He could just feel a pulse. "Let's get a stokes-basket in here!" O'Queef shouted out of the room. A stokes was passed up the stairs, from outside the front door, and into the room. Bootknife was carefully lifted and placed into the basket. As soon as the straps were buckled, he was pushed out the door and passed downstairs to where the Paramedics and ambulances were waiting.

As soon as Bootknife had been removed from the room, they pulled Killa out from under the slab the same way. Killa was in a little better shape than Bootknife. He curled his body into a ball almost as soon as he heard the crack. He was right below the window at that time, so he was up against the wall, which is one of the best places to be in a collapse. When they had him out from under the slab, his helmet and mask both had a crack in them. He still had a little air left in his bottle and he was actually breathing, although he was unconscious. The stokes-basket that was used to bring Slim out was handed up the stairs and slid into the room. The Tower's crew placed him in it, strapped him in, and four of them carried him out of the room and down the stairs. On their way out, O'Queef told L.T. and Loo, to shut the line down and to back out of the building.

Outside, CPR was being done on Bootknife and the Paramedics were inserting an ET Tube into his throat so they could establish an airway. Killa was immediately thrown into the back of an ambulance and sent to the hospital. The Paramedics had been working on Bootknife for about five minutes when they got a good pulse back. His oxygen saturation levels still weren't good and the carbon monoxide level was extremely high, so the ET Tube was left in. Once they got him stabilized they loaded him into the back of the ambulance, and he was taken to the landing zone for the med-evac helicopter. While they were working on getting him out, the Chief had requested the med-evac helicopter in case they were needed. Once there, they off loaded him from the ambulance, put him on the helicopter, and he was flown to the closest trauma center.

Hose lines were set up outside the house and an exterior attack was made until the fire had been extinguished. No other lives were going to be risked on this house.

Chapter 13

When the med-evac helicopter landed at the trauma center, Bootknife was taken to the Emergency Room for a quick evaluation. X-rays showed both legs were shattered, his left hip was fractured, two vertebrae were chipped, his left arm was broken in eight places, his collarbone was broken, his skull was fractured, and he had some minor internal bleeding. A CT scan was done on his head and it showed he had minor bruising on the brain. He was a mess, but he was still alive. A surgeon was on standby in the operating room, awaiting his arrival. Hospital security was standing at all the major hallways intersections to stop foot traffic so the doctors could get Bootknife to the surgeon without delay.

The fire crews remained at the scene of the River Street fire for approximately two hours after Bootknife, Killa, and Slim had been transported to the hospital. When the Chief left the scene, he drove right up to the trauma center. Slim and Killa were taken to the same hospital as Bootknife, which was good because they would be together. When the apparatus cleared from the scene, it was very strange for Big Deve, Doc, and Domer to ride back in Engine 5 knowing half of their crew was missing. Their broken helmets and other various items of gear, which had been removed prior to them being transported, were sitting on three of the seats in the back. Domer couldn't look at those seats. He glanced at them once and immediately started tearing up. It had been an extremely emotional day so far, and they still had to wait to hear about how the three were doing.

At the firehouse, Engine 5 was taken out of service due to the amount of hose that needed to be replaced, as well as because of the tools that were missing from it. No one wanted to touch the personal items that were in the back belonging to Slim, Killa, and Bootknife. Avon's Engine stopped at the firehouse after clearing from the scene and volunteered to provide coverage for the Hosers since they had three brothers in the hospital. There were a lot of guys walking around the bays with the thousand-yard stare, completely in shock. Many had tears welled up in their eyes, and they were doing everything they could to keep the floodgates from opening up. Smeagle was quietly consoling Meagle who was really taking the whole event hard. Assistant Chief Higs told Doc, L.T., and Loo to leave as soon as they put their gear away. They had enough people to get things cleaned up. His crew from Engine 3 had been assigned to cover Hose Company 1, and they were already working on getting the rigs put back into service.

"Beamer, can you give L.T., Loo, and Doc a ride to the trauma center? I don't want them driving." Higs asked.

"Absolutely! Come on." Beamer said. Bootknife was as much a brother to him as he was to Loo and Doc, so he had no problem driving them. He also wanted to get up there so he could be there for Bootknife's parents.

"Thanks Beamer!" Doc said. It was all he could muster up at that time.

The car ride to the trauma center was eerily quiet. L.T., Loo, and Doc just stared out their windows the whole time. Visions of the collapse played in their heads continuously. It was like a never-ending nightmare. When they arrived at the trauma center, Beamer dropped Loo and Doc off at the entrance to the Emergency Room and L.T. said that he would stay with Beamer while he parked the car. Doc and Loo walked into the waiting room and saw the Chief there with their Mom,

Dad, and Stepmom. Killa's family was sitting there as well. His father was still in his uniform because he got the news while at his firehouse. Slim's family was sitting in the corner. Everyone had been crying since before Doc and Loo walked in, but as soon as everyone saw them walk in, they really began balling their eyes out. Their parents got up and ran to them and began hugging them as tight as they could. They almost lost one son, so they weren't letting the other two go. Doc finally was able to convince them to all sit back down again. He and the Chief were trying to keep everyone thinking positively when Beamer and L.T. came into the room. They immediately went to work consoling all the parents.

A doctor walked in about an hour later. All eyes were on him. He told Killa's family that he was in stable condition and was being transferred to a room for observation. He had a broken shoulder and a mild concussion. He was in the best shape out of the three of them. Killa's family found out what room he was going to be in and asked if either Bootknife or Slim were going to be able to be placed in the same room. The doctor told them he would see what he could arrange, depending on the condition of the other two. He also notified Bootknife's and Slim's family that both were still in surgery and that he would give them more information when it became available. Killa's family felt bad leaving everyone in the waiting room, since they had all been so supportive to each other, but they had to see their son. Everyone understood.

L.T. and Doc were becoming a little antsy by the three-hour mark. They had not been given an update on either Bootknife or Slim since the doctor came in with Killa's update. About twenty minutes later, the same doctor walked in with the surgeon who had been working on Slim. They told Slim's family that they had gotten him stabilized and had completed the surgery. He had to have three plates put into his leg, due to the severity of the breaks. He also had a fractured collarbone, both eardrums were ruptured, and had to have more than fifty stitches to close up the lacerations on his face from his mask breaking. The ER doctor worked some magic and was able to get Slim into the same room as Killa.

The Chief and Bootknife's family were growing tired in the waiting room a couple hours later, when they were informed that Bootknife was still in surgery. He was doing well, but the injuries he sustained required a lot of work to fix. After getting that news, Doc and L.T. decided they were going to go up to see Slim and Killa. Bootknife's parents hadn't eaten since they arrived at the hospital, so the Chief told them to take some time and get some food. He would call them if anyone came with news. Bootknife's parents were a little hesitant but finally decided to go to the cafeteria.

When L.T. and Doc got to Killa and Slim's room, both were awake and talking to their parents. L.T. knocked on the door and poked his head in. "Got room for two more at this party?" he said laughing a little.

"L.T.! Get your ass in here." Killa said, still a little out of it.

L.T. and Doc stepped into the room and closed the door behind them. Both Killa and Slim looked like they were in decent shape. Slim couldn't hear well so Doc found some paper and a pen and wrote down what he wanted to say to him. They didn't stay too long because they could see Slim and Killa were getting tired. They said farewell and headed back to the waiting room. When they got to the waiting room, Bootknife's parents had just gotten back from the cafeteria. No new news had come yet on Bootknife's condition. L.T. and Doc took a seat in the corner of the room, and they both eventually nodded off.

L.T. and Doc had been asleep for two hours or so when Bootknife's surgeon came into the waiting room. The Chief woke the two of them up and stood up waiting for what the surgeon had to say. He knew Bootknife had been in really bad shape when the med-evac took him from the scene. He was preparing for the worst news but hoping for the best.

"I come with good news," the surgeon said. "It took quite a while to piece things back together, but we have him stable. He's going to remain in critical condition though. We're putting him up in the ICU tonight to keep an eye on him, but as long as he does well through the night, we'll get him to a regular room mid morning tomorrow."

A huge sigh of relief was let out by everyone. "Will we be able to see him tonight?" asked Bootknife's mother.

"Yeah. I think I can get a couple of you back there for a few minutes." said the surgeon.

Bootknife's mother and father went back to see him, as well as the Chief. Bootknife's mother broke down when she saw her son. He was covered in bandages and casts. He had tubes and wires coming out of everywhere and was still sedated. When she got to the side of his bed, she squeezed his hand and gave him a kiss on his cheek. She leaned down next to his right ear and whispered, "Hang in there, son! You are so strong and so brave. You need to pull through because both of your nieces and your nephew need you! I love you and will be back here first thing in the morning." She kissed him again, and Bootknife's father helped her out of the room after speaking a few quick words into his other ear.

The Chief had waited for Bootknife's parents to exit before he walked up to the side of the bed. He stood there choking back tears, looking him over from head to toe. He rested his hands on the bed rail and looked back up at his face. The parts that didn't have bandages on them were black and blue and swollen. "Bootknife, you crazy bastard! You need to get better soon! We need you back at the firehouse. I got word a little while ago that the two boys you and Killa rescued survived. Don't you give up!" He patted the back of Bootknife's right hand, turned around and walked out of the room. As soon as he was clear of the door, the floodgates opened and the tears ran down his face. He got himself composed as he rounded the corner into the waiting room. He wished Bootknife's family the best and told them to call him if they needed anything. After that he left, promising to be back the next day to check in on him.

Chapter 14

Two days later, Killa was released from the trauma center. He was going to be out of service for six weeks while his shoulder healed. After six weeks, he'd be able to be placed on light duty while he completed physical therapy. He was relieved to be out of the hospital. On his way home, he had his parents drive him to firehouse so he could see Beamer, Grey, and Big'n'Rich. When he walked through the front door, he found all three of them sitting in the office, working on some paperwork. "What's up maaaannn?!" he said, catching all three of them off guard.

"Holy shit! What's going on bud?" Grey asked, getting up to shake his hand.

"Heeeyyy. How's it going?" asked Big'n'Rich.

"Good, you?" Killa responded. He adjusted his sling as he walked into the office to shake everyone's hand.

"You just get out?" asked Grey.

"Yeah. They let me out on good behavior," Killa said laughing.

"Fucking guy!" Beamer said laughing with the other two. "You get any of those nurses' numbers?"

"Yeah, I got a couple. One of them was sending me pics of her last night," Killa replied proudly, with a huge shit-eating grin on his face.

Killa stayed long enough to get the latest news from them. The fires had stopped and things were back to normal. They had had a couple medical calls the day before and had one fire alarm early that morning. Killa glanced out the window and saw his mother looked like she wanted to get home, so he said bye to them and left.

A day later, Slim gave Killa a call, on his way home. "Yo bitch! I'm out!" said Slim when Killa picked up.

"Yeah maaaannnn! You're fucking crazy man! Looking like some kind of a scar-faced animal, maaaannn!!"

"Fuckin' A, right!" replied Slim.

"How's Bootknife doing?"

"He's coming along. He's still in ICU, but Doc stopped by before I left and said they were probably going to be moving him to a recovery room in a day or so."

"Damn man! He's one tough son of a bitch. I don't think I would have survived if I was in his place," Killa started thinking about the moment after he heard the crack of the ceiling coming down. "You know, the last thing I remember before getting hit by the ceiling was Bootknife pushing me into the wall."

"Really? There's no doubt about it. He is one tough bastard. Must be the Marine in him. You know, both of your grabs made it right?"

"Yeah. The Chief told me the day after, when he came to visit."

"Good shit man! Congrats!" Slim was just pulling up to his house, so he told Killa he'd call him later, then hung up. Domer and Farley were in the driveway waiting to help get him into his house. Slim's mother had gone to get his prescriptions, and his father needed to make sure the dog didn't get under foot as Slim came inside. Domer and Farley helped get Slim's wheelchair into the house and wheeled him to his living room. His parents had set up the couch to sleep on so he didn't have to try to climb upstairs to his room. They helped him out of the chair and onto the couch.

"Fuckin' A, Slim! Hopefully you lose some weight while you're healing," Domer said, breathing heavily. "This is the second time I had to carry your fat ass into your house! Next time you better be lighter."

Slim and Farley started laughing. "Just remember my philosophy," Slim responded. "It takes a real man to build a shed over his tool!"

Once Slim was all settled in, Farley and Domer left. They both headed down to the firehouse to see the Savage. He was working overtime for the last two hours at Hose Company 1. There were a few cars in the parking lot when they pulled in at the firehouse. L.T. and Doc were out front talking to Shakes, and Savage was in the office putting the last couple calls into the computer system.

"What's up, you savage beast?" Farley said to Savage, standing in the doorway.

"Hey! What's going on you Mongolian Mountain Goat?"

"Just got back from Slim's house. We helped him get into his house and settled in, in his living room."

"Nice man!" Savage said in his gravelly voice. "How's he doing? Yeah, and what about the Killa and Bootknife?"

Domer answered before Farley, "Killa got home yesterday and seems to be doing pretty good. Bootknife is still in the trauma center. He's in the ICU still."

"No shit? I should go see Bootknife on my way home tonight. I didn't realize he was still in the ICU."

"Both Domer and I were thinking about going up there tonight, so if you want, we'll go with you," said Farley.

"Yeeeaaahhh Man! I don't know if I could face seeing him like that alone."

"Yeah, I haven't been up to see him for the same reason," said Farley.

"Me either," followed Domer.

"We'll go see the beast tonight then." Savage turned back to the computer and kept punching away at the keyboard. He wanted to get all the paperwork done so Beamer wouldn't have to worry about any of it in the morning.

Domer went into the meeting room and changed the channel on the TV, pulling up the tractor pull championships, while Farley went out front for a smoke and to talk to Doc to see how Bootknife was doing. Doc was sitting on the front bumper of Engine 5. He looked exhausted, with big bags below his eyes. He'd been at the hospital since Sunday, leaving just long enough to shower and change at home. He told Farley that Bootknife really hasn't been responsive to anyone who's come to see him. "The doctors have kept him heavily sedated, ever since the surgery. It's still looking like they are going to move him out of the ICU in a couple days, but that's only if he keeps improving." Doc continued to explain to Farley, "Vera has been there since she got the call, on her way home Sunday. She's a mess right now. I think if it wasn't for her friends calling and supporting her, she probably would have had a complete melt down."

"Damn. I bet. It can't be easy on any of you! I know I still can't get over that this happened!" said Farley, taking the last two drags on his cigarette then pushing it into the dispenser. "Do you guys need anything?"

"Big Deve took care of my Mom's lawn and Bootknife's. My Aunts have made a bunch of meals and froze them so my Mom wouldn't have to cook anything. I think the best thing you could do is just come and see him as much as possible."

"Domer, Savage and I are going to go up and see him at five, when the Savage gets out of work. If you guys end up needing anything just give me a call. It doesn't matter what time it is."

"Thanks man. We will. Well, time to go home and shower and grab a little shut eye before I head back up to the trauma center. I'll see you guys later." Doc stuck his head in through the front door and said bye to Savage, then he got in his car and left.

"I guess I'll get going as well. Got to get a short nap in before work tonight," said L.T. He threw up a wave and headed out.

Shakes and Farley walked inside and joined Domer in the meeting room. At five o'clock, Savage grabbed his personal effects and locked up the firehouse. Domer and Shakes climbed into Farley's truck, and they followed Savage up to the trauma center. As they pulled into the parking lot at the trauma center they passed Big'n'Rich. They returned his wave, and then they spent a couple minutes searching for spot to park. After finding two spots next to each other, they got out of their vehicles, looked at each other, looked up at the tall trauma center, and then started walking towards the main entrance.

Inside, the trauma center was bustling with activity. Nurses and doctors were moving about quickly, while families walked in groups up and down the hallways and through the open lobby. Savage and Farley glanced around the area for any signs that would direct them the right way to the elevators. Bootknife was on the third floor ICU, and the four of them didn't feel much like taking the stairs. After looking for a couple minutes, finally Shakes spotted the sign and led the group towards the elevators. When they reached the third floor, the sign on the wall in front of the elevator doors showed the ICU to the right. They followed the hallway signs, taking two lefts then a right. Once they were through the double doors and into the ICU, they had to look at every room window they passed to find the correct room. Farley had just passed the room when Shakes saw Beamer and Grey.

"Over here you dumb ass," whispered Shakes, laughing at Farley being such an airhead.

"Don't call me a dumb ass, dumb ass," Farley fired back.

"Cut the shit, guys," Domer said with a disappointed look on his face. He knew they were just messing around, but they were there to see their brother, and instead of acting like adults, they were acting like children.

Domer led the way into the room, followed by Savage, and Farley and Shakes bringing up the rear. Savage stopped dead in his tracks when he got past the curtain and saw Bootknife. He was in complete shock. He knew Bootknife was hurt badly, but he didn't expect to see him like this. Bootknife was hooked up to a couple different monitors. He had one IV going into his right arm and another going into the back of his left hand. When Savage got himself composed, he walked to the left side of the bed and rested his hands on the bed rail. After staring at Bootknife's swollen face for a couple minutes, he turned his head to look at Beamer and said, "This dude's a beast! Look at him. Casts on both legs, and left arm, bandages covering his head, face swollen…he's tougher than anyone I know."

"Tell me about it bro!" replied Beamer.

When Savage looked back at Bootknife, he saw his eyelids were opening. "Bootknife. Can you hear me buddy?"

Bootknife blinked a few times and looked up at Savage. Weakly, he got out, "What are you staring at you Bulgarian Lot Lizard?"

"You crazy ape! Welcome back!!" responded Savage.

Grey got up and ran to the nurses' station. The first nurse he saw he tugged on her arm and said, "Bootknife's awake!"

They ran into the room to find everyone laughing. The nurse walked up and stood next to Savage. She looked Bootknife over then said, "Welcome back. How are you feeling?"

Bootknife looked into the young nurse's eyes and said, "You aren't a dancer are you? You look familiar."

All the guys in the room laughed hysterically. They all knew he had put a few women through college with the amount of money he had dropped at the strip clubs over the years. "No," the nurse said, "I left that all in the past. The doctor will be in shortly." She winked at him and walked out. Everyone's eyes went right to her ass as she walked out. Her tight skirt really defined her ass, and it was hard for them not to stare.

"I knew it! Damn my memory is still good!" Bootknife said, with a little more animated voice. His whole body was sore, but it was bearable with the medication they were still pumping into him. Beamer had just gotten off the phone with Bootknife's mother when the doctor came in to examine Bootknife now that he was awake. He was young as well. He couldn't have been more than thirty years old, but he looked no older than 14. Bootknife picked up on it and stared at him. As the doctor left, Bootknife asked, "What's with all the young medical professionals around here?"

"I don't know," said Beamer, "but I'm not complaining about the view. The nurses here have to be some of the hottest ones I've seen yet."

"You got that right! Is Killa still here? He'd have a couple of them in his bed every night if he was," said Bootknife, laughing. He laughed because he knew it was true. Killa was a man-whore and he wasn't afraid to admit it.

Bootknife's parents and Vera showed up about fifteen or twenty minutes after Beamer had talked to Bootknife's mom. They were all excited to see that he was awake now. Especially Vera, who had been waiting ever so patiently to be able to give him a kiss and have him kiss her back. The next day, Bootknife was moved into a recovery room, where he spent the next two weeks while he healed up and started his rehabilitation. When he left the trauma center, he was sent to a rehab facility, where he remained for five months.

Chapter 15

It was a bitterly cold December day when Vera walked into Bootknife's room at the rehabilitation center, with a huge smile on her face. She was there to bring Bootknife home. Over the five months that he had been there, he had all of his casts removed and had been doing physical therapy everyday to build up his leg strength. He had lost a lot of muscle mass while lying in bed at the trauma center, so he had to slowly build it back up and start walking again. He used a cane when he walked, and had a little limp, but he was leaps and bounds ahead of where he should have been. Vera gave him a kiss as he zipped up his luggage and said, "Got everything?"

"Yup, I think so."

"Okaaayyyy. We're not turning around to come back here if you forget something. Once we walk out of those doors, we aren't looking back."

"I know. Believe me, I'm ready to get out of this joint," said Bootknife, kissing her back.

Vera grabbed one of his bags off of the bed, and he grabbed the other. They walked out of the room and down the hall into the lobby. Christmas music was playing over the speakers, creating a cheerful atmosphere. Staff members were moving around with their assigned tasks for the day. From behind them came a woman's voice, "Bootknife! You weren't thinking about leaving without saying good-bye to me were you?"

Bootknife and Vera turned around to see Katie, his physical therapist, walking towards them. They had spent almost every day together for the last five months, but he had completely forgotten to stop by her office earlier that day. He lied, "Of course I wasn't."

"I know you wouldn't. So, how are you feeling today?"

"Ah, my back is a little stiff and my hip is a little achy, but I'll get over it."

"Don't be a tough guy. Remember to keep doing those exercises I gave you."

"I will. I will," Bootknife said with a sly smile on his face.

"I hope you two have a Merry Christmas and an even Happier New Year." She gave both Vera and Bootknife a hug, and then stepped back. She had to turn her head and wipe the tears from her eyes. She had built a strong personal relationship with both of them. She had only been a physical therapist for two years, but Bootknife had been the best patient she had had so far. She saw the Marine in him come out in every session. When most people would have given up or slack off, he constantly gave 110%. She admired that and had looked forward to every session.

"Thank you and the same to you!" Bootknife replied.

"Take care of yourself, and make sure you stop by and visit me every once in a while; both of you."

"We will! Thanks for everything you've done for me, for us. I really can't thank you enough," said Bootknife, wrapping his arm around Vera's shoulders.

Bootknife and Vera hugged her again, turned around, and walked outside. When they reached Vera's car, Bootknife put both bags into the back seat and got into the passenger seat, letting Vera drive. There weren't very many cars on the road, so the trip home was quick. When they got back to Bootknife's house, they went right upstairs and began unpacking. Bootknife stopped unpacking to look around his room. Vera caught his gaze as he looked out the window, into the backyard. She could tell he was happy to finally be home.

"I'm happy you're home," Vera said to him.

"I'm happy to be home. Thanks for standing by me while I got better. It really means the world to me!"

"You's welcome shorty," Vera said laughing.

"Are you ready for tonight?"

"Absolutely! I have to run home quick to grab my dress though."

"Well, I think I can handle putting the rest of this away, so run and get it."

"Okay." Vera walked around to the other side of the bed, to where he was standing and hugged him. She kissed him long and hard on the lips. "I'll be back in a few. Don't get into any trouble while I'm gone."

"I can't promise, but I'll try not to." Bootknife smiled at her and kissed her again. "Run along now," he said.

Vera stared into his eyes for a few seconds, smiling, and then walked out of the room. Bootknife finished pulling everything out of his second bag, dividing all of his clothes up by what drawer they went into. After he put everything away, he went to his closet to make sure his suit had been dry-cleaned. It was too late to do anything about it if it hadn't been cleaned, but he was in luck, his suit was hanging there still wrapped in the plastic cleaner's bag. Under his suit, on the floor, were his dress shoes. They were a little scuffed and dusty, so he picked them up, grabbed his shoe shine kit from the nightstand, and went downstairs to shine them up.

Vera walked through the front door as Bootknife was putting the finishing touches on his shoes. She was holding her dress up in front of her so it wouldn't drag on the ground, and didn't even see him sitting on the couch as she walked by. He thought it was weird that she didn't acknowledge him when she came in, so he got up and followed her upstairs.

"Oh Fuck! You scared me!" she said, clutching her chest.

"Hahaha, sorry," he said. "I didn't mean to."

"Where did you come from?" she asked still trying to catch her breath a little.

"I was downstairs on the couch shining my shoes. You walked right by me."

"Sorry. I was in my own little world when I came in."

"I could see that. I like that dress. You's gonna look sooooo seeessssyyy in that!" Bootknife said with a grin from ear to ear.

"Oh thanks," she said.

She had that look in her eye that she used to get all the time, and Bootknife picked up on it immediately. He looked at the clock on the nightstand. It was 3:45, so they had a couple of hours before they had to be at the Clubhouse for the firehouse Christmas party. Bootknife gave her the same look, closing the bedroom door as he walked towards her. "It has been six months…" he said, cutting the sentence short.

Bootknife's phone was ringing when he walked into his room from the shower. He looked at the caller I.D. before he answered it. "What's up Slim?"

"What up mother fucker? Where you at?"

"I just got out of the shower and trying to get dressed."

"You better hurry the fuck up and get to the party! They're extending Happy Hour so you need to get here so we can get some drinks in you!"

"Yeah, yeah. I'm hurrying, but it's kind of hard to get dressed and talk to you at the same time. Give me a few minutes and I'll be there. Okay?"

"Hurry it up! Bye."

Bootknife looked at Vera who had a quizzical look on her face. "Slim. He's three sheets to the wind and telling me to hurry up and get there."

The quizzical look on Vera's face turned straight to a look of astonishment. "Shit! He's drunk already?"

"Yeah!" Bootknife said laughing. "Good thing we only have to go across the street."

They finished getting dressed, made sure the house was locked up then went downstairs. When Bootknife opened the garage door he saw that snow was falling and there was a dusting on the ground already. He really wanted to take his car, but with it being rear wheel drive with 425 horsepower, it wasn't really good in the snow. He looked back at Vera and asked, "Can we take your car? It's much better in the snow."

"Of course, but can you drive it?"

"Yeah. No problem."

He took the keys from her and carefully led her to the car. They took a right out of his driveway, drove a hundred feet up the road and turned left into the condo complex where the Clubhouse was. After parking the car, Bootknife helped Vera out of the car and they walked into the building. Christmas music and people talking and laughing could be heard coming from upstairs where the banquet hall was. When they reached the top of the stairs, Slim saw them through the window and came stumbling over to open the door. Bootknife saw him coming and stopped Vera so she wouldn't get hit by the door.

When Slim hit the door, it swung open wildly. "Bootknife! You crazy mothafucka! Get your ass in here! Here, take this beer!"

Slim forced himself between Bootknife and Vera, wrapped his arms around both of their shoulders and escorted them into the room. Everyone was on their feet clapping. The Chief ran up to the DJ and grabbed the microphone from him and announced Bootknife's arrival. "The man of the evening has arrived! Fresh from the rehabilitation center!"

Bootknife began to blush. He threw his right hand into the air and gave everyone a wave. Slim moved out from between Vera and Bootknife and walked to the two seats he'd been saving for them. Bootknife, using his cane, walked through the crowd shaking everyone's hand, and made his way to where Slim was. He set his beer down on the table and shook the Chief's hand when he walked up to him. "Merry Christmas Bootknife! We're glad you made it tonight!"

"Thanks Chief! I've been looking forward to this night for the last couple weeks!"

The Chief gave Vera a hug, "Merry Christmas Vera!"

"Merry Christmas Chief!"

Killa came up and handed Bootknife another beer and stuck out his hand, "Merry Christmas Maaaaannnnnn!"

Bootknife shook Killa's hand and pulled him in and hugged him, slapping him on the back a couple times. "Merry Christmas Bro!"

Bootknife pulled one seat out for Vera, so she could sit down then he sat down himself. Bootknife took a long drag on the beer Slim gave him, draining half the bottle before setting it down on the table. "Ahhhhhh, that's good! I've been looking forward to that!"

"Whoa, Whoa! Slow down you drunk!" Slim said laughing.

"I've got to catch up with you!" Bootknife said grinning.

He took one more drag, emptying the bottle. He set it down on the table in front of him and asked Vera what she wanted to drink. Bootknife, Slim, and Killa all got up from the table and headed to the bar to get drinks for their dates. When they came back to the table, the Chief announced, "Dinner's served!"

Bootknife, Vera, and the rest of their table waited for a couple tables to get up and get in line before they made their way over to the serving line. The members and their significant others, who were in line behind them, came up and shook Bootknife's hand. They told him they were glad to see him and wished him and Vera a Merry Christmas. Dessert was being prepared as everyone was finishing their meals. The banquet staff came around to all of the tables and passed out the soufflés. The best part of the evening was about to begin.

Chapter 16

When the banquet staff came around again to collect all of the dirty plates, the three Chiefs got up from their seats and made their way over to the table set up on the side of the dance floor. The Chief got the microphone from the DJ and turned it on. He began his speech.

"Good evening! Merry Christmas to everyone! For those of you who don't know me, I'm the Chief here at Hose Company One and to my right are the Assistant Chief and Deputy Chief. I hope everyone enjoyed this great meal. Let me start by saying thank you to the banquet hall and staff for putting on this event. Although we call this our Awards night or Christmas party, it's really more of an evening to thank our wives, girlfriends, and significant others for putting up with us running out on them all year. Being Volunteers, we can be called at anytime, day or night, to respond to help our neighbors. While we're gone, our loved ones are left behind. We may think we have a tough job, but they have the toughest of all, and we can't thank them enough for the sacrifices they make to keep things running smoothly at home while we're gone."

The Chief paused long enough to clear his throat and look at his note cards. "This year was a busy year. It was a record breaking year as well. We ran more calls this year than ever before, we made more money at the carnival this year than ever before, and we broke the record for number of members who signed the Constitution in one year. Although this year has been a successful one for the department, it came close to facing tragedy. Back in June, three of our brothers almost paid the ultimate sacrifice in a collapse at an early morning fire. Luckily the crews on scene acted swiftly and proficiently, and were able to rescue the downed firefighters and get them to the hospital where they received the care they required. Up until a couple days ago, I thought only two of the three were going to be here tonight. Luckily though, things went well and the third was released from the rehabilitation center today, and was able to make it here tonight. Those three firefighters were Killa, Slim, and Bootknife. If you three could please stand."

Killa, Slim, and Bootknife pushed their seats back and stood up. Everyone in attendance was clapping and cheering. There were even a few wet eyes in the crowd. All three of them threw everyone a wave and sat back down. Vera took Bootknife's hand in hers and squeezed it. At the same time she leaned and kissed him on the cheek. She whispered in his ear, "You made it baby!" Then she sat back as the Chief began speaking again.

"As I said before, tonight is to honor our loved ones who make sacrifices every day. But, tonight we also use this time to recognize those members who have gone above and beyond during the year at both calls and training. And with that, we'll start the awards."

The first awards to be given out were the Recognition Awards. These awards were to recognize members who worked at the bigger calls during the year, fires, bad car accidents, etc. Bootknife, was one of the few who had been around for all of the calls that fell under the recognition award. In years past, this award was a framed letter that had a write up with each person's individual actions at each call recognized. To save money, and to class it up a bit, two years before, the award became a nice plaque with Hose Company #1 across the top, Recognition Award written in the middle, and the year on the bottom. It was a standard plaque just personalized with each member's name under the year. Since multiple calls were being recognized that year, each member getting this award only got one plaque. Like Slim, Bootknife wasn't a huge fan of these, because he felt they were a little impersonal, but he understood why they changed the award. About fifteen calls were being recognized this year, which included the week of fires. By the end, almost every member was up front. There were only a few members still at the tables, and they were mostly the older guys who didn't go on the rigs for calls anymore.

After all of the recognition awards were given out, everyone sat back down. Vera asked to see the plaque as soon as Bootknife got back to the table. "That's a nice plaque baby! That'll look really good on you wall with the others."

"Yeah, I guess. It's kind of a bullshit award." Bootknife tried to say it quietly. One of the new guys in the department was sitting right behind him, and was really excited that he got an award.

He must not have said it too quietly though because Slim heard him and leaned to his left, toward Vera, and said, "Fuckin', A man! This will look great in my fireplace."

Vera elbowed Slim and said, "Stop that! You guys earned that award. You should be proud."

"We don't need awards to know we did a good job," Bootknife said to Vera smiling.

Vera elbowed Bootknife now and just glared at him. The Chief started talking again. "The next awards tonight are for a few members who went above and beyond the call of duty on three of the calls we had this year. The first set of awards, go to three members who saved a child who had fallen into a pool at the beginning of May. On arrival, these members found the child floating face down, on top of the water under a warming cover. They arrived on scene within three minutes of dispatch, and risking their own lives, two of them jumped in to swim under the cover to get the young boy. They began CPR as soon as they exited the water, and were able to revive him before the next units arrived. They are being awarded the Meritorious Service Award tonight. The three firefighters are Chachi, Bootknife, and Slim." Bootknife and Slim stood up slowly, looked over at Chachi, nodded at each other and made their way up to receive their plaques. These plaques were more personal. They actually had the date of the call and a short two line explanation of what they did.

When Bootknife and Slim sat back down, Vera had already moved all of the stuff in front of their spot at the table so they had a place to set their awards. "The second set of Meritorious Service Awards tonight is being awarded to two firefighters who rescued a young boy from a fire in June. The fire was in the evening on Londonberry Place. These two firefighters found the boy in his room unconscious and not breathing. Their exit was cut off by fire, after a hose length burst and was unable to control the fire while they were searching. Remaining calm and focused, they called for the RIT team to set up a ladder and assist with removing the victim through the window. After getting the boy out, these two firefighters were forced to bail out through the window just seconds before the room flashed over. The boy was revived and is alive today because of these two firefighters' actions. The two firefighters are Bristol and Bootknife."

The room erupted in applause as Bristol and Bootknife made their way up to the Chief to receive their plaques. On the way up, Bootknife was getting a pat on the back by almost everyone he walked by. After posing for a quick picture with the Chief, they both sat went back to their tables and sat down. Vera had a smile from ear to ear when Bootknife looked over at her. She was gazing at him with a look of amazement. She really enjoyed seeing her man be recognized for the things he does, although Bootknife would be just as content with having someone simply say, "Good work."

Bootknife placed the third plaque on top of the others, kissed Vera on the cheek, and looked back at the Chief. "The final set of Meritorious Service Awards being awarded tonight, are for the last fire in the week long stretch of fires. It happened on River Street and has become the worst fire I have ever been to. That morning, three of our best firefighters became trapped after a series of collapses occurred on both the first and the second floors. This all happened after two children had been rescued from their second floor bedroom. Both children ended up surviving because of their actions. The three firefighters who are being awarded this Meritorious Service Award are Slim, Killa, and

Bootknife. We are extremely lucky to have all three of them with us tonight."

As Killa, Slim, and Bootknife rose from their table, the room once again erupted into applause. Eventually by the time they got up to the Chief, everyone was on their feet giving them a standing ovation. People with cameras flooded to the front to get pictures of the Chief awarding these three guys. When the picture taking was done, Killa, Slim, and Bootknife made their way back to their table, shaking everybody's hands along the way. Vera was still standing when they reached the table. She threw her arms around his neck and gave him a kiss. Slim was behind Vera making faces at Bootknife and saying, "Awwwwwwwwwww."

Bootknife looked at Slim and said laughing, "Shut the fuck up!"

Bootknife put the plaque down on top of the others and sat back down. The Chief had five more awards left to give out, "The next award is the Rookie of the Year award. This goes to a firefighter with less than two years who has excelled in training and on calls. The member being awarded Rookie of the Year finished his Firefighter II and has taken three other courses during the year. He also has shown me and the other officers in the department that he can complete tasks on the fireground with little supervision. He has gotten a lot of experience over the last year with the number of calls he has made, so this year the award goes to Killa."

Killa looked extremely surprised to hear his name. It took him a few seconds to realize that he needed to stand up and get his award. When he sat back down he leaned in and said to everyone at the table, "Really? I figured someone else would have gotten this."

Bootknife looked at him and said, "Bro, you were the only rookie who deserved that. The other rookies weren't around for shit and haven't done any further training since Fire I or Fire II." Bootknife extended his hand and shook Killa's.

The Chief picked up the next award and began speaking, "The next award is the Firefighter of the Year award. This is similar to the Rookie of the Year award, but it's for the members who have two years or more in the department. This year, we had a few guys that were qualified candidates for this award. It was an extremely tough decision, but we were able to narrow it down to one. This member has already been up here a couple times tonight. He was on more than seventy-five percent of the calls that were recognized tonight with the Recognition Award, and he was even on a couple of the Meritorious Service calls. He obtained his Q-endorsement, has been cleared on two of the rigs at the firehouse, and will be cleared on the third in a couple days. This year's Firefighter of the Year is Slim."

Bootknife slapped Slim on the back as he was getting up to receive his award. Bootknife leaned into Vera and said, "He's deserved that award for the last two years! I'm glad they finally got their heads out of their asses and gave it to him this year!"

When Slim got back to the table, Bootknife stood up and shook his hand, before he sat down. "That's been your award for the last two years. It's about time you got that!" Bootknife said to him.

"Haha, thanks man," Slim responded.

The last three awards were Best Use of Technical Skills, which went to Bootknife, Top Responder, which went to the Assistant Chief, and the Chief's Award went to Bristol for leading the RIT team the day of the River Street fire. At the conclusion of the awards, the Chief thanked everyone again for coming and told everyone to hang around because the best part of the night was about to begin. Pointing at the DJ, the Chief said, "DJ, spin that shit!" The DJ started the music, and people immediately started getting up from their tables and made their way to the dance floor.

Bootknife stood up from his chair and stretched. "I'm heading to the bar to grab another drink. Vera, you want anything?" Vera shook her head. "Slim, Killa, anyone need another drink?" Slim and Killa both nodded their heads and got up to walk up to the bar with Bootknife.

"Three Bud Lights, please," Bootknife said to the bartender.

Bootknife threw a five-dollar bill up on the bar as a tip. He took two of the bottles and handed them to Slim and Killa. He turned around and grabbed the last bottle. He faced Slim and Killa and proposed a toast. "Here's to a year of pulling kids from pools and fighting fires! Oh, and here's to bow legged women!"

Slim and Killa laughed. "Fuckin' A, man!" they both responded, tapping the necks of their bottles together.

Bootknife took a long swig of his beer and looked out at the dance floor. Forever by Chris Brown was blaring over the speakers, and the girls were out there dancing. Vera caught him looking at her and smiled. He winked at her and took another swig of his beer. Vera tapped Slim's girl and pointed over at the three of them. They then started motioning that they wanted the three guys to get out there with them and show them their moves. Slim wasn't intoxicated enough to start dancing yet, and Killa was too busy flirting with the bartender, so Bootknife handed Slim his beer and limped out to them. "Sha…Sha…Sha…Shake that ass!" He said putting his arms around Slim's girl and Vera. Both girls laughed and slapped his ass, playfully.

"Whoa! Easy does it!" yelled Slim, laughing on the edge of the dance floor.

Bootknife was known for his dancing skills before he was injured. He wasn't sure how he was going to do, but he ended up still having it. More members joined him on the dance floor after seeing he still had his dance skills. After the DJ played The Cupid Shuffle, he slowed it down a bit and played Don't Stop Believing by Journey. Slim ended up making his way out to the dance floor for that song. He handed Bootknife his beer and began dancing with his girl.

Vera wrapped her arms around Bootknife, looked up at him, and smiled. She hugged him hard. When she released her hug, Bootknife looked into her eyes. "Thanks for putting up with me for the last year," he said.

A little confused, she asked, "What do you mean babe?"

"Well, I had a lot of time to think while in the hospital and I realized that it can't be easy for you to watch me run out on you for calls all the time. I'm sure you understand why I have to leave, but I just want to apologize for putting strangers ahead of you."

"Stop," she said. "I'm so proud of you! I'm so proud of all of you guys! I may be scared to death when you run out for fires and some of the more dangerous sounding calls, but I know that you have a lot of good guys watching your back so I know you'll be fine. Now, six months ago, that was a little different, but look at how that turned out! Your friends saved your life and I can't thank them enough!"

"I know. And thanks for all of the support you've given me. What I'm trying to say is…well, I think Pitbull put it best, 'For all we know we might not get tomorrow. Let's do it tonight!'"

Vera laughed, "Oh, you silver tongued devil, you!" She laid her head on his shoulder and hugged him again. "Don't you ever die! I need my Local Yokel!"

"Six months ago, fire couldn't kill me, so I think you'll have to suffer with me for a few more years at least."

"Okay," she said giggling a little. "That's good."

Chapter 17

It didn't take long for disaster to strike Hose Company 1 again. This time it would be tragic. A of couple weeks after Bootknife went back on active duty, he responded to an early morning motor vehicle accident on Rescue 15. Big Deve positioned the Rescue behind the accident scene. The ambulance was already there and the EMTs were in the car evaluating the patient. The guys began getting off the rig to go to work. Loo, Slim, Doc, and Shakes stepped off the Rescue on the officer side. Bootknife was getting out on the opposite side, but had to wait for one of the new guys, Snake Shit, to get out first. Snake Shit swung the rear driver side door open. As his left foot hit the ground, Bootknife saw the flash of headlights and heard the door slam against the side of the rig.

"Oh Fuck!" Bootknife whispered to himself. He quickly looked to the left to see if any other cars were coming, then jumped out of the truck. When he looked to his right he saw a car racing down the street and Snake Shit lying motionless in the middle of the road ten feet away. "Noooooooooo!" he yelled as he ran to the kid's side.

Loo heard the commotion from the other side of the rig and came around to see what was going on. He saw Big Deve jumping out of the driver seat running towards Bootknife who was kneeling in the middle of the street.

"Snake Shit's been hit!" Big Deve screamed to Loo.

Loo got on the radio, "Rescue Fifteen to Base! Firefighter down! I repeat, Firefighter down! Hit and run! Start me a second ambulance and Paramedics, get me the Med-Evac helicopter, and get me an Engine from Headquarters! The vehicle is a white Honda, heading West on the Avenue at a high rate of speed!"

Loo grabbed the second medical bag and oxygen case. He told Doc to check with the ambulance to find out if they needed help, and if they were set to get over to help with Snake Shit. He ran with the bags to Bootknife and Big Deve. Big Deve was holding c-spine on Snake Shit and Bootknife was working on cutting Snake Shit's gear off. When Loo got up to them, he saw Snake Shit had frothy blood coming out of his mouth, a massive laceration to his head, and was unconscious.

"Shakes! Get the suction!!" Loo yelled. He opened the oxygen case and started sizing up oral airways. As soon as Shakes got there with the suction, he started clearing the blood from Snake Shit's mouth, inserted the airway, and began ventilation with a bag valve mask.

Doc ran back from the car, "What do you need? The ambulance has everything under control over there."

Bootknife had just finished a rapid assessment on Snake Shit and found multiple broken bones on his left side. He checked for a pulse, "He's in arrest. Start CPR!"

Doc kneeled next to Snake Shit and began chest compressions. Loo looked at Shakes, "Get me the collars, a longboard, and the AED. I'll take care of suctioning."

Shakes ran back to the rig and grabbed the collar bag, slung the AED over his shoulder, and ran to the other side to grab a longboard. Slim had just finished putting speedy dry down and gotten back to the Rescue to help Shakes. They set everything down behind Loo and pulled out a c-collar. Engine 4 and Medic 16 were calling Loo over the radio. Loo grabbed Slim and said, "Take over bagging him for me." Slim took over and Shakes got the longboard positioned, while Bootknife put the collar on Snake Shit to stabilize his neck.

"Rescue Fifteen to Engine Four, set up the landing zone at the High School. Medic Sixteen if you don't have a driver for Engine Two, bring who you have to the scene, in the Medic." Loo distanced himself from his crew so he could let them work.

Bootknife took over as the Lead EMT on Snake Shit. "Doc how you doin' on compressions?"

"I'm good for now. I'll switch as soon as we get him on the board."

Bootknife acknowledged what Doc said, "Okay. Slim, keep suctioning as needed. Shakes, get the long board set. We're rolling on Big Deve's count."

Big Deve looked at everyone, "Ready? On Three. One, Two, Three."

Doc stopped compressions and helped Bootknife roll Snake Shit onto his right side. Shakes slid the longboard under his back and said, "Set!"

Again Big Deve said, "On Three. One, Two, Three."

Doc and Bootknife rolled Snake Shit onto the board, adjusted him quickly so he was centered, then had Shaken take over on compressions. Doc began strapping Snake Shit to the board while Bootknife set up the AED and got the pads placed on him. Doc just finished securing Snake Shit's head when the AED was ready to analyze. Everyone cleared away from Snake Shit and let the AED analyze. There was no shock advised so Shakes started chest compressions again. Doc took over ventilating Snake Shit, and Slim moved next to Shakes so he would be right there when Shakes needed a break. Bootknife began dressing the laceration on Snake Shit's head with a large trauma pad when the second ambulance arrived with the Paramedics.

Bootknife gave the Paramedics a report of his findings and the actions they had taken as they were walking up to the scene. Loo radioed dispatch and notified them that the first ambulance had departed with a transport. He also radioed Engine 4 and told them to notify the Med-Evac crew that the Paramedics and the Patient would be headed their way in a few minutes. As soon as the Paramedics got an advanced airway into Snake Shit and had given him some drugs to try to get his heart started again, they loaded him into the ambulance and took off for the landing zone. Loo radioed Engine 4 and told them the ambulance was headed to them. Engine 4's officer responded back that the Med-Evac helicopter had just landed.

When Medic 16 arrived, Loo told them to remain in service at the scene in case there were any other medical calls. The Police Department took over the scene at that point so they could take photos and conduct their investigation. Rescue 15's crew remained at the scene for three hours before they were finally able to clear. When they returned to the station, they were given the news that Snake Shit didn't make it. They pronounced him upon arrival at the hospital.

Slim, Shakes, Loo, Doc, Bootknife, and Big Deve were still pretty shaken up about Snake Shit's death a couple days later. A critical stress debriefing team had been called in to talk with 15's crew, but it didn't help much. Bootknife took it the hardest, seeing how he witnessed the whole thing. The State Police caught the driver just over the line in the next town. The driver's blood alcohol content was twice the legal limit. All six of the guys that were on the Rescue that morning wanted to go beat that guy within an inch of his life, but held back because they knew it wouldn't bring Snake Shit back.

Slim, Shakes, and Bootknife hung the mourning bunting up on the firehouse and lowered the flag to half-mast, as soon as they had gotten the news upon returning to the station. Snake Shit was given full fire department honors at his funeral. Doc and Slim worked with the Chief and had a large memorial plaque made up, with Snake Shit's picture on it, and hung it up in the meeting room.

After a couple weeks, things started to get back to normal at Hose Company 1. Bootknife had stopped beating himself up over the whole ordeal and moved on with his life. Slim eventually got his sense of humor back and started picking on everyone as he used to. The damage to the Rescue was repaired and a small brass plaque was mounted to the side of the cab, in between the driver's door and the rear door, commemorating the life of Snake Shit. The department held a memorial ceremony every year on the date that Snake Shit was killed.

All wounds heal with time though, and this case wasn't any different. Although their brother was gone, he was not forgotten.

THE END